OTHER SIDE

Ray Hollar-Gregory

AUTHOR'S NOTE
This book is a work of fiction. Names, characters, places, and incidents either are the product of the author's imagination or are used fictitiously, and any resemblance to actual persons, living or dead, business establishments, events or locales is entirely coincidental.

ISBN: 0997544805
ISBN 13: 9780997544800

To my family

TABLE OF CONTENTS

INTRODUCTION

Jordan Baros sought an honorable, purposeful existence. He followed his conscience, listened to his inner voices, rationally debated the conflicts, and applied intuition to his decisions. But he was aware of his frailties and did not always do the "right thing." He acknowledged his commitments and personal needs and measured the outcome by levels of engagement and satisfaction. He managed risk with prudence until he didn't. Jordan achieved career respect and made relationship choices. It was a complex set of small and large pieces, an interminable mosaic.

The responsibilities he met as a father and husband provided fond memories that spoke loudly: the boys playing together in the yard on a weatherworn swing set as he looked out from the kitchen window, family portraits hanging on the winding staircase wall and sitting on mantels over the numerous fireplaces, social and business dinners that built friendships and career, and the personal sacrifices he made—not for himself but for the good of his family.

In spite of Jordan's diligence in meeting his obligations, he was conflicted. There was the other side. He sought validation in complex ways and found his impulses irresistible. He was driven and let consequential forces, including contradictions, paradoxes, and hypocrisy flow, each a part of his and everyone else's riddle.

CHAPTER ONE

My wife, Trina, was Ivy League–educated, with a degree in communications from Cornell. She had worked in public relations and media advertising until the birth of our boys, Jared and Chad. Call it melancholy, despair, or depression, but she had been unstable the past few years. Initially, her doctor had indicated postpartum depression, but our youngest was now five years old, and Trina's behavior had persisted and worsened. She cried a lot and was quick to anger, and her nerves were on edge. Cooking burns, broken water glasses, forgetfulness, and disorder verging on hoarding were symptomatic of her stress level. Sex was infrequent, occurring somewhere between her not being interested and me not being too tired.

Don't get me wrong—I love my wife. And unless you count flirting, fantasizing, or contemplating a parallel universe as cheating, I was innocent and had never crossed the loyalty threshold. Never can be ephemeral, but I'm getting ahead of myself.

One day about midweek in the late 1980s before cell phones and Internet, I returned to my office from a meeting and retrieved a message to call the emergency room of Mountain Hospital immediately. It had been raining since early the previous evening, and it was now just after midday. An ominous thought crossed through my mind because of the word *immediately* in the message. Had Trina done something unthinkable? Had something happened to Jared or Chad? I called the number and was told that Trina was in an auto accident, and I should go to the hospital.

I left work and headed to Penn Station to catch the train back to Jersey and go to the hospital. About an hour later, I walked into the hospital, approached the triage desk, and inquired about Trina Baros. The nurse took a moment to look up Trina's information and directed me to the room where Trina was resting. I followed the directions down the hallway with its antiseptic scent until I reached her room. She was lying on her back, slightly propped up in a blue hospital gown. She had a neck brace, a gauze bandage around her forehead, and an elastic bandage on her left wrist and arm. She reacted with relief and subdued joy when I walked in. Before I could say anything, Trina started to apologize.

"I'm so sorry I was in an accident, and the car is in the shop...I don't know how it happened."

"Don't worry about it. Are you all right?"

Trina indicated that she had a slight concussion and had cut her head when she hit the steering wheel. They were going to take x-rays of the wrist to make sure there was no fracture, and her neck and shoulder hurt, but it was nothing serious.

"The police came and took all the information and towed the car to an auto body shop," she said. I had recently purchased a BMW 5 Series, in addition to an SUV we owned.

"Don't worry about the car. They'll fix it, and we'll get a rental until then," I said.

I tried to comfort her as best I could and met with the attending physician to get the official diagnosis and plans for her discharge.

"I'd like to hold her for about forty-eight hours, as a precautionary measure. She took a pretty good hit to the head," he said.

I agreed and returned to Trina to let her know what was happening.

"I can't stay here," she said.

"You have to. This could be serious. Plus, there's nothing you can do at home. The kids will be fine for the next two days...they can stay with your mother for the two days."

She didn't feel good about the situation, but with no other choice, she agreed. I sensed that she was feeling mellow from the Valium the nurse had administered. After a couple of hours, I collected her clothes and promised to bring others and some personal items later.

"Okay, I'm going now...to get the boys situated and let everyone know you're all right—not completely all right, but you'll be fine in a few weeks." I kissed Trina on the cheek and left the hospital.

I was concerned for Trina and knew the accident was a result of all that was happening in our life—her deferred career, my demanding one, and the stress of child-rearing. The next day, I sat in my office looking out at Central Park's Sheep Meadow Bay, where just last year we had dinner in the office, covertly shared a bottle of wine, and watched Diana Ross's concert in the park while listening to simulcast on WBLS. The fact that a thunderstorm disrupted the concert made the experience from the office that much more enjoyable.

The boys were staying with my in-laws. I called my friend Maria and told her I wanted to see her after work. She agreed and asked if I wanted something special for dinner.

"Surprise me but save room for dessert," I said.

"I have something sweet for you," Maria said with a teasing tone.

CHAPTER TWO

I've known Maria Velez for about two years. We had started as friends. Since her move to Brooklyn last year, we have been intimate lovers. We talk frequently, at least once a day. A couple of times, when schedules allowed, we traveled together on my business trips. Maria also worked in advertising on the creative side. We had not been together for a while, so I was looking forward to the evening.

I arrived at her apartment in Park Slope, Brooklyn, after taking the #1 subway from midtown. Her apartment was part of the changing Park Slope area, which was going through early changes associated with gentrification and was attracting a mix of young professionals. The neighborhood was strikingly diverse. When I got off the train and entered the streets in Flatbush, the people I saw were mostly West Indian and Latin, sprinkled with a few professional suit types, particularly between six and seven thirty in the evening. After walking a few blocks south of Flatbush, I observed the obvious changes. The sights and sounds caused me to abruptly retune from the third-world Caribbean/Latin colorful mosaic to a relatively banal yuppie impression. It all added to the flavor of New York and was exciting and adventurous.

Maria moved from Jersey after her photographer boyfriend kicked her out of his house. He had become suspicious and wire-tapped the phones, uncovering a series of salacious conversations and rendezvous plans between her and a lover. Her lover dropped her off late one evening a block from her house after the two had gone out to dinner, and spent time together in a hotel on the Jersey side of the Hudson overlooking the shimmering New York skyline. When she arrived home, Andre, her boyfriend, was waiting. He forced her to listen to the wiretapped recordings of her plans for that evening, as well as other conversations. He beat and slapped her while calling her all types of names, including slut and whore. After sodomizing and raping her, he told her to pack her belongings and be out of the house by the end of the week.

Thinking back, I recall that day when we first met. She boarded the same train I take to work from New Jersey to New York. It was late April, and the weather was making a dramatic and permanent shift to spring. All things spring, including the shedding of outer clothing, were blossoming. The season's change heightened my hibernated winter senses. I first noticed her on the train platform. She was wearing a tapered, white cotton dress with a colorful op-art-inspired print, drawn in at the waist with a red patent-leather belt. The dress was about two inches above the knee and was set off by matching red high heels. She presented a striking figure accentuated with sexy flair. I boarded the train before her and was seated when she entered. The train was fairly full, and she sashayed down the narrow aisle looking for the first empty seat. I couldn't help but notice and followed her every move. When she found an empty seat, she shifted her weight from one hip to the other while continuing to gymnastically balance herself on those Wizard of Oz ruby-red shoes as if on a balance beam. Finally, she twisted her body at the hips to squeeze into the opening beside the woman occupying an aisle seat. The suspense concluded when she placed her round apple shaped bottom in the available window seat. I smiled to myself and felt like standing and flashing a placard showing a perfect ten, but I controlled my urges.

I obsessed over how I would get to know her, but I didn't have to wait long. The beauty of public commuting is the timing and predictability, knowing the time each morning when she would take the train. All I had to do was to be there and wait for the opportunity to introduce myself. Strategic planning? Stalking? Guilty? Yes!

A few days later, I gathered the nerve to execute my plan. Like an alley cat in a tough neighborhood, I sized up my prey, stalked from a distance, and was poised to pounce. I felt the rush as I approached her outside Penn Station, when we both exited the building and headed uptown toward our respective jobs. I maneuvered through the morning crowd and came from behind her, to her right side.

"Hi. How are you?"

"Fine," she responded, looking up while trying to determine who I was but not recognizing the face.

"I've seen you at the Mountain Top Station and on the train. I live in town; you live there?"

"We moved in about nine months ago. How 'bout you?"

"A few years," I replied, after hesitating to speculate on what "we" meant, having scoped out earlier that she was not wearing a wedding ring.

"How do you like it?" I asked.

"I don't. I sleep there but spend the majority of my time in New York. Then again, I look forward to leaving the city after a rough week to enjoy the slower pace and take time to recharge before the next week. You know what I mean?"

"Yeah, I hear you, I love the city—the energy, the people. Everything has me wired...being here every day is relatively new. I worked in Jersey for years, confined to either a city under revitalization or stuck in a suburban office complex in the middle of nowhere, eating lunch at a local diner or pizzeria. And now it's Fifth Avenue, Rockefeller Center, Saks, the Village…I had lunch at Top of the Sixes the other day and drinks at B. Smith's after work."

"You are quite the man about town, aren't you?" Maria said.

We continued to chat until I reached my destination.

"Well, this is me," I said.

"Oh. I'm a few blocks farther east. You haven't told me what company you work for?" Maria said, making the statement a question.

"I work for Federal Retail Corporation. They have stores mostly in the Southeast and West. They compete in the luxury retail niche against Neiman Marcus, Bloomingdale's, and Saks."

"And what do you do?"

"I handle financial services. They have a couple of insurance companies, corporate financings, acquisitions and mergers, and diversified interests for the company…pretty dull stuff compared to the criminal trials I used to do."

"But I'm sure it pays well." Maria seemed to admire my silk suit, business loafers, and Burberry trench coat. Not overstated, but a natural blend appropriate for a lawyer.

"It allows for a few more luxuries."

"Good for you."

"I'll see you around," I said as I entered the building.

"That was nice," I thought. I could tell from that moment that nature was challenging my moral convictions. Different from flirting or friendship, there was an urge to possess. And after we eventually crossed the threshold, the subsequent transgressions were with less frequent feelings of guilt or moral reflection.

⊶≺╪ ╪≻⊷

Maria lived on the second floor of a building that contained eight co-op units; she buzzed me in, and once upstairs, I rang the bell.

She met me at the door, the pleasant bouquet of her perfume reaching me before she did. Her small co-op was a railroad apartment; it had a long hallway ending in a small living room. The kitchen was located off the hallway, as were the bedroom and bathroom. She was sensuously dressed in a beige teddy cut high on her thighs, her shiny hair hanging long, and her shapely legs flowing nicely down to her peach high pumps. The shoes accentuated her body lines—particularly her breasts and booty.

We embraced gently; I think she could sense my eagerness. I was ready to unleash my passion right in the entranceway, but Maria had other ideas.

"I have a surprise for you, *papi*," she said and led me by the hand to the kitchen. She took the lid off one of the simmering pots that contained *camarones* in a white-wine sauce that she intended to serve over yellow rice.

"That smells delicious," I said and kissed her sweetly on the back of the neck.

"Look inside the fridge and get the wine."

Without hesitation I got the wine, a dry white Italian pinot grigio. I struggled to open the bottle with the erotic, phallus-like corkscrew she gave me. She laughed at my awkwardness and positioned herself between the bottle and me as we stood, with her buttocks softly touching my groin. She gently placed the corkscrew on top of the bottle, inserted the cone-shaped tool into the bottle's opening, and broke the cork's seal.

"I hope the rest of the evening is as rewarding," she said coquettishly after having dislodged the cork.

"It will be," I said. "I have a surprise for you." I pulled out my little brown bottle with the gold coke spoon attached. I dipped it gently and gave her a hit and took one myself to smooth the edges. Her eyes sparkled, and like an alto sax in a small café, we blended with the harmony of the moment.

"You are so bad; I love it. I would have never thought when I met you...you were like this. You were 'all lawyer' and stuff. I figured you to be some preppy, self-absorbed, about-the-résumé kinda guy. But you are genuine. I guess that's why we get along."

"Thanks. I think?"

"It's a compliment," Maria said.

She finished cooking and set the table. I sipped my wine, shared a couple more hits with her, and enjoyed the substance, vision, and lightness of being.

"Do you hear from your ex anymore?" I asked, speaking about Andre.

"Last time I spoke to him was about getting some things I had left. He threatened to give them away if I didn't come pick them up."

"Did you get them?"

"No. I don't want to see him. You know how crazy he was after he found out about what I told you. He was always weird, but he became frightening near the end. I never told you this, but after I left, I spoke to one of Andre's friends, a guy named Doug, who worked with him. He told me that Andre had bought a gun and wanted to confront my friend."

"That's interesting," I thought. I was glad I waited until after she left him before we started dating.

Getting a little agitated, Maria said, "I don't want to think about him. He's crazy and probably would have done something like that a few months ago, but it's my understanding that he's moving on. He intends to sell the house. I wonder if I can get the part of the down payment I gave him?"

"Was your name on the deed?"

"No. Why didn't you advise me, Mr. Lawyer?"

"I didn't know you that way back then," I said, as if taking her seriously.

"No palimony. Lost down payment. I blew that one, didn't I? Enough about the past. Let's talk about us."

We eventually settled down to enjoy our dinner. Besides the shrimp and rice, there was a salad made with romaine lettuce, black olives, and feta cheese and a vinaigrette dressing—it blended nicely with the mood.

During dinner, Maria and I talked casually about our careers, her job with an advertising firm, and her dissatisfaction about the lack of opportunities and recognition, despite her accomplishments. Although the financial benefits of my present job clearly outweighed my former job as a district attorney, I missed the rough-and-tumble of criminal trials. I recounted to Maria one case in which I prosecuted a young drug lord and was threatened by members of the gang. As a result, I was assigned a bodyguard and eventually obtained a permit to have a gun at my residence.

"I've come a long way from those days...at least, now I don't have to worry about anyone threatening my life if I miss a comma in a corporate bond prospectus review." Changing the subject, I asked, "How's your mother doing?" Maria's mother, Carmen, had breast cancer.

"Not so well. She is weak, and her hair is thinning from the chemo. We speak every day, but it's tough. My sister is struggling to raise her own family and care for Mom. I don't know what we're going to do. These last few years have emotionally drained me. It's tough to lose a parent and to watch another struggle with cancer. You know, Papa didn't leave much, and she has no medical coverage. Thank God for Medicare, but that doesn't cover prescriptions. Going back and forth to Jersey for medical visits isn't easy...I don't know what I'll do if things get worse."

"It must be tough. I lost my grandmother, and that hurt. We were close, but I've not dealt with the loss of a parent or other serious illness in my family. Thank God. It must put you in touch with your own mortality."

"Yeah, I guess longevity is not in my cards."

"Why do you say that? You'll be healthy for years and probably still fresh at sixty."

"We can hope I'm still walking—forget the fresh," Maria said, without looking up from her plate.

"Ummm, that would be freaky. I've got this thing for grannies."

"You are a sick man."

Maria got up from her seat and sat on my lap and kissed me affectionately on the mouth. "I want to shove these dishes on the floor and let you fuck me right on this table."

With no verbal response, I kissed her. Our lips parted, and my hands explored the tender smoothness of her thighs. My primal urges surfaced, and I reached out and slid the thin strap of her silk teddy off her shoulder. She instinctively raised her arm, bending it at the elbow to free and expose her beckoning left breast. She removed the strap from the other side and was totally bare from the waist up—bare breasted and exposed, verbally silent but communicative through her seductive eyes and facial expressions. I opened my shirt to expose my broad bare chest and pulled her gently toward me until her nipples made contact with mine. We continued to arouse and excite one another; Maria's nipples were not at all shy or timid and responded in sign language to the slightest contact. They were full and proportionately ample, now swollen with excitement. Her broad Latina shoulders accentuated their prominence. I kissed her, and she rubbed against me and thrust her body into mine.

Speaking softly, I said, "Let me have all of you babe...you give me so much...I want to give it back."

I wanted her totally. My moist mouth and saliva-laden tongue savored Maria's unblemished beauty. I kissed her forehead, eyelids, and lashes, slowly and gently etching love markings on her skin. I continued to kiss and lick her neck and earlobes, making my way to the cleft between her bountiful and fully engorged breasts. Having licked her, I retraced the journey of my mouth and tongue with delicate strokes of my fingers, simultaneously licking her hard, protruding nipples and the pinkish-brown areolas the size of silver dollars that surrounded them. The sight reminded me of something I overheard my grandfather say to a group of male friends sitting on the front porch one afternoon. He declared that you can measure a woman's sexual intensity by the size of her areolas—the bigger they are, the more intense the desire. Maria's arms were now covered with minuscule goosebumps, and her body squirmed passionately on my lap. I eased her off my lap, and we both stood up and embraced. I caressed the curvature of her rounded hips and indented waist as her teddy fell silently onto the kitchen floor, and then I effortlessly lifted her and placed her on the granite kitchen countertop.

"That's cold, baby," she said.

"Only for a moment," I said softly.

Her legs were spread apart, and the pinkish-red tender lips of her vagina were inches from my mouth as I assumed a seat in the chair I had previously occupied. Maria was completely open and quickly forgot the initial sensation of the cold granite countertop. Without hesitation, my tongue penetrated deeply into her moist opening. Slowly and repetitiously, I removed my tongue from inside her to trace the outer edges of her pussy, ending those traces by softly stoking her clit with my tongue while my lips covered her vagina lips, just as I had similarly done on her erect nipples moments before. Maria was beside herself. Her chesty baritone moans had a distinguishable cadence and indicated increasing levels of pleasure. She held my head with a hand on each side, seeking to draw my face deeper inside her. I got up from the chair and held my thick penis, which was as hard and pulsating as Maria's nipples. I moved closer to share my passion and need with her.

After a while, Maria cooed like a baby. "*Papi, mi amo*, my baby, cum inside my *chocha*." Our bodies moved together, sensuously with elegant grace and Afro-Latin rhythms. She felt as feminine as I did masculine, and we came together that evening entangled, amorous, and oblivious to the world.

I lost count of the times we climaxed—it was a pleasure being with her.

CHAPTER THREE

I had arranged to leave work early the next day. Trina was being released from the hospital later that afternoon, and I would pick her up around three o'clock. I called Maria late that morning to thank her for the prior evening.

"Hey, babe, how ya doin'?"

"Fine, now that I heard from you...how's things with my Jersey man?"

"That's typical New York arrogance, but you know Jersey is the best-kept secret, and your garden can't get enough of the state."

"You nasty man...¿*Que pasa*? What's happening? When you comin' back?"

"Missing you, baby. Still feeling you. It was sweet last night... honey, that was so great. You are silk and then some."

"I was getting a little concerned these past few weeks; I thought you might be avoiding me," Maria teased. "I was hoping I didn't put too much on you last night...I know how fragile your fine ass is."

"Fine ass, yes. Fragile? No! Remind me to show you fragile next time I'm lovin' you and I have to cover your mouth so the neighbors don't call the cops. I'll pleasingly hurt you the next time I see you."

"And when might that be? I haven't seen you in a few hours... and how's the wifey doing?"

"That's why I'm calling. You know, Trina had the accident. She's pretty banged up; her neck is in a brace, she has a concussion, and she sprained her wrist. She's been in the hospital the past two days. I'm picking her up this afternoon to take her home."

"I didn't know she was hurt that badly. When we spoke yesterday, I thought it was a minor accident."

"She'll be okay. It's mainly precautionary stuff because of the neck and head. With everything that's going on, it has been crazy lately. But we'll talk soon. I have things to tell you."

"What?"

"We'll talk...now's not the time."

"You fuck me, call the next day, and tell me the wife is in the hospital and there's something else you need to tell me but can't... what am I supposed to do in the meantime? What's going on? Are you all right? When do you plan to tell me? You've got me all confused right now! When can I see you?"

"Today I can't," I said.

"I know you can't today. When?"

"Okay, I'll call you. Trust me—everything is fine...it's cool. We'll talk; you'll see."

"Whateevveerr!" Maria said in an irritated tone. "I'll be here; you do what you have to. Call me later if you get a chance."

"Right. We'll talk later. Be good."

"See you later. No, you be good."

Unable to focus on work, I called Trina at the hospital. "How you doing?" Without waiting for an answer, I asked, "Has the doctor seen you yet?"

"I'm sore and didn't sleep well. The nurses were in here all night waking me up for tests or to give me some medicine. I have to sleep on my back, and if I move a certain way, I get a pain in my arm. I need to get home so I can get some rest. The doctor will be here at one, and then I'll be ready to go. What time can you get here?"

"I'll leave the office in a couple of hours; I drove in today. Anything I need to bring?"

"Yeah, can you go by the house and get my sneakers and sweat suit, the black one? I think it's in the closet hanging up, okay?"

"Okay. I'll see you in around three. If you think of something else, leave a message at home. Have you spoken to the boys at your mother's?"

"I spoke to my mother last night; everybody's fine. My mother wanted to bring them home tonight, but I told her to bring them tomorrow, when June gets back. I forgot she had to report to immigration today and won't be back until tomorrow. My mother is getting old; she can't watch the kids so long. I don't know what I'd do without June—not just because of the housekeeping, but for everything else she does. She said she would stay over if we needed."

"Try to rest; I'll see you in a little bit."

"Don't forget the sneakers and clothes. And Jordan...uh...I'll tell you later."

I didn't want to get into anything heavy at the moment and could tell from her tone that she was headed there. "We've got a lot to talk about after you get well." We both knew it was inevitable and overdue.

"I know. Bye."

"Bye."

I arrived at the hospital promptly around three that afternoon after going home to get Trina's clothes and shoes. I walked to the visitors' desk and got a pass and then took the elevator to the fifth floor, got off, and headed straight down the long, wide hallway to Trina's room. As I turned the corner, I heard the distinct voice of Hazel, my mother-in-law, coming from inside Trina's room. Momentarily I hesitated, not expecting Hazel to be there. Gathering composure, I turned into the room to see not just Hazel, but my father-in-law, George, and my sons, Chad and Jared.

Chad looked straight at me and exclaimed, "Daddy's here, Mommy!" Jared, my younger son, stopped what he was doing and ran across the hospital room into my outreached arms. Chad followed suit, and we had a huge group hug. I kissed and lifted each of them up separately and then together as I twirled them both around the room.

"Where's my boys at?" I repeated several times as the merry-go-round continued. Jared, in his cute, youthful, innocent way, answered my rhetorical question. "We here, Daddy...we here, Daddy."

Finally, I gently let them down and bent over to be face-to-face with them. Jared, out of nowhere, punched me right in the shoulder.

"Ouch," I said, feigning pain, and put up my fists in defense against the attack that both sons now began to unleash.

Trina had seen enough at that point and intervened. "You boys, stop...be quiet. Let your father in so we can get ready to go. This is a hospital, not the playground!"

The boys stopped. After gaining composure, I looked at Hazel and said, "Hi, Hazel. I didn't know you were coming." Before Hazel could answer, I nervously turned and looked at George. "How ya doin', Doc?"

"Hey, Jordan, where have you been?" George said. "We've been waiting for you."

"I had to stop by the house to get Trina's shoes and clothes. Took me longer than I thought. I told Trina I would be here at three."

Hazel had no expression on her face but nodded to acknowledge my presence. "We decided to come. The boys wanted to see their mother...we weren't sure if you would be able to get here."

I didn't know how to take the comment. We had always had a strange relationship. Trina's parents were first-generation southern Negroes, who had migrated north to seek a better life for themselves and were products of Jim Crow segregation, the Depression, black self-hatred, and all the other neuroses that result from racism and economic deprivation. George served two years in the navy during the Korean War and had later gone to Morehouse University and Meharry Medical College, both on the GI Bill. After med school, George married Hazel, and they moved to New Jersey, where he set up a successful medical practice. George and Hazel were part of a small, close-knit association of black bourgeois, predominantly composed of professional graduates (lawyers, doctors, and dentists) of one of the historical black colleges. George and Hazel enjoyed a black upper-middle-class lifestyle and its privileges, both real and assumed, and spent their summers with their counterparts in Oaks Bluff, Martha's Vineyard.

Trina benefited from her father's hard work and success. She attended private schools and was driven by Hazel's hopes for Trina to have more than she ever had. Hazel had wanted Trina to marry into a family of prominence...specifically Calvin Henderson, the son of one of Hazel's physician friends, Dr. Jack Henderson, a well-to-do orthopedic physician. Calvin loved Trina and pursued her throughout college while she was at Cornell and he attended Brown. They were close to engagement until I showed up. The insults and slights Hazel inflicted on me during courtship were still raw. Hazel conspired with Calvin's mother to undermine Trina's relationship with me in the hopes that their plans for a prearranged marriage for Trina and Calvin might happen. I was invariably insulted at social affairs and house parties that Trina's parents hosted when the Hendersons were present.

Hazel would amiably parade Calvin around, introducing him to her friends and reciting his accomplishments—Ivy League schooling, father's prominence, doctor's son, and so on. I never felt the same level of exuberance coming from Hazel when she introduced me to friends. In spite of Hazel's gaming, I never saw Calvin as a formidable threat to Trina's affections for me. For one thing, Trina let me know he wasn't a threat, through her actions and words. Furthermore, I had conceded that Calvin's SAT scores were better than mine, but Calvin scored poorly on other factors. Physically not that attractive, he was an egg-shaped guy, whose waistline and chest were the same measurements, and he had a fair, yellowish complexion with blue-green veins that were transparent through his skin. His blackness was the lowest quotient of melon required—the one-drop measurement. His straight hair lacked style, and he wore khakis and loafers. To me, he lacked the cool gene. Calvin was a clone with no individuality; he was raised to be his father.

I'm more independent and was raised differently, with challenges and no safety net or preordained map for success. Certain traits such as charisma, interpersonal skills, and intuition are not easily measured on standardized tests. The ability to walk into a room and assess the dynamics and the people and position oneself to win—these are the intangible things that gave me confidence in spite of Hazel's preemptive attitude. Ironically, despite Calvin's admirable credentials, he always seemed intimidated by me.

I responded to Hazel's greeting. "Well, thanks. You never know what traffic is going to be like trying to get out of New York."

Trina jumped in at that point. "Hi, Daddy," she said, a reference she used for me around the boys.

"Hi. Here's your sweats and sneakers." I placed them on the bed. "How ya feeling?" I looked at Trina's arm, which was in a white sling.

"Okay, I guess. I can't do anything with my arm. The neck is better, but I have to wear the brace at night. The doctor says my cuts will heal. I have to come back in a few days to get the stitches removed."

"You ready? Did the doctor discharge you?" I asked.

"Yeah, I'm ready. Let me change into the sweats, and we can go. Bring the car to the front, and take some of these things down. Be careful with the flowers." Trina had received flowers from friends and family. There was even a bouquet from Calvin.

CHAPTER FOUR

My company, Federal Retail Inc., besides being a retail conglomerate, was diversified in financial services. It owned a life and casualty insurance company and used direct marketing to target its retail credit card holders to successfully sell its insurance products. I recently took over lead responsibility for execution of the legal aspects of the business strategy to expand financial-services offerings to include stocks, bonds, and mutual funds. This particular assignment required me to establish a money-market fund for Federal's credit card holders. The nature of the deal required an expert understanding of the Securities and Exchange Act, Investment Advisors Act, and various state "blue sky" laws to protect consumers against unscrupulous broker dealers. This was a tremendous opportunity. My boss, Ted Doran, was a hard-nosed Irish attorney, who reminded people of Ted Kennedy. During my interview, he implied that affirmative action policies were challenging the company's hiring practices, and sometimes the best people for the job were discriminated against.

"Now, don't get me wrong. I'm confident in your legal skills, and your prior accomplishments are top-notch," I remember Ted saying.

I was confused with this double-talk. How encouraging it would have been if he had expressed himself more as a mentor than an adversary by saying something like, "Jordan, I'm going to expect as much from you as the other attorneys within this department, if not more. I say this because of the misperceptions that may exist before they know you—their prejudices. It is my intent to challenge and push you every day—to make you a first-rate corporate lawyer and provide you the support and resources to achieve that objective. The only thing I ask in return is that you dedicate yourself to this partnership, work hard, and prove the racial skeptics wrong."

I was determined as a black man and professional to succeed, to achieve due recognition for my efforts and work product, and to disprove what can't be proven.

⎯⎯⎯⎯

Winthrop & Hudson was Federal's primary outside counsel and would be assisting me with the project. I entered their building for a meeting in lower Manhattan on Wall Street feeling that my new assignment was just the challenge I hoped for, and I knew all eyes were on me. I also knew that, given the state of my personal life, things would be more difficult to manage. Luckily, I possess the ability to compartmentalize things. I can prioritize, organize, and direct the necessary energy to do the things that have to get done. I can manage my emotions and passions and call up my rational and objective self to accomplish the goal or task I face. It's like two separate brains turning on and off.

The transformation had begun and intensified as I approached the stately offices of Winthrop & Hudson. The richness of the oak-paneled office was immediately apparent upon entering the reception area. Original Early American paintings, forest-green leather furniture, a spiral staircase leading to upper-level offices, and oriental rugs projected old-money wealth. The firm was founded in the late eighteen hundreds; corporate financing, mergers, and acquisitions had always been part of its work. It was one of the leading firms during the Industrial Revolution, supporting European and domestic bankers and financiers, and it continued in that role, representing some of the largest Fortune 100 companies in the world. It had offices around the world and four hundred lawyers.

Undaunted, I made my way to the reception desk, and in my most professional manner and tone, introduced myself to an extremely attractive blonde, who could have easily, if she chose, been at Ford Models or Wilhelmina Models instead of Winthrop & Hudson.

"Hello, my name is Jordan Baros. I'm with Federal Retail Corporation and have a two o'clock appointment with Mr. Lawrence Whitney."

She smiled back at me with exceptional sapphire anime eyes. "Thank you, Mr. Baros. I'll let Mr. Whitney know you are here. Please take a seat. I'm sure his assistant will be right with you."

After about two or three minutes, a matronly, older woman appeared and approached me, extending her hand and introducing herself as Mr. Whitney's administrative assistant, Miss Gilliam. She led me to a small conference room, where Mr. Whitney and another man were waiting. Both stood up as I entered. Miss Gilliam did the introductions; the other man's name was John Billings, an expert in securities law. Mr. Whitney's legal expertise was in financial services and banking. Both men extended their hands when we were introduced. Miss Gilliam indicated there were soft drinks and coffee on the ornate credenza against the wall and then left the room.

"Well, Jordan—I can call you Jordan?" Mr. Whitney said.

"I prefer that. Thank you, Lawrence."

"How's my good friend Ted doing?" Lawrence asked.

"He's doing well and sends his regards."

"We go back a long way. You know, we were classmates at Harvard."

"No, I didn't realize that." I knew Ted had attended Harvard, but he failed to mention that Lawrence was a classmate.

"Yes, Ted went to work for the U.S. Attorney, Southern District, and I took a clerkship with District Court Judge Sherlock, who later became an appeals court judge for the Second Circuit. I remember in his second year with the U.S. Attorney, he argued a motion before Judge Sherlock, and he was good. Ted was always well prepared, but he was new, and the judge didn't give him a break that day. Challenged him on every point and case he cited. You could tell halfway through his presentation Ted wanted to turn around and run out the courtroom. You could see the sweat beads on his brow. I wanted to walk over and hand him a handkerchief. But Ted hung in there, and before it was over, you could see the tide turning. The judge never said it, but I think he admired Ted's tenacity. It was like an initiation into a fraternity, and Ted passed the hazing. Later, when he came before the judge, it was completely different; he would joke with Ted, bring him into chambers, and tell war stories. I think Ted established a better relationship than I did with the judge, and I clerked for him for two years!"

Without taking a breath or a pause, Lawrence Whitney shifted the discussion to the business at hand. "Enough of my tales. What about you, Jordan? How long have you been at Federal?"

"Almost two years now," I said. Anticipating the next question, I told him how much I enjoyed the work and presented some of the projects I was involved with. I had developed a two-minute talking-point drill that was concise and to the point for situations like this.

Feeling it was a good time to redirect the discussion and assert myself, I began by saying, "Gentlemen, as you know, Federal is very interested in expanding its financial offerings. From a business perspective, Federal has done well with its other financial-service offerings, particularly the life insurance products. A feasibility study found growing consumer demand for equity investing, both full-service and discount brokering activity, with an expectation to double in the next five years, with margins in the twelve to fifteen percent range. With interest rates in the eighteen percent range, money-market funds are the best investment vehicle for consumers right now—high return, no risk. This is a new direction for Federal but offers a great opportunity for diversification and a strong ROI. Specifically, the fund could benefit the company in several ways: For example, the company could form subsidiaries, which for a fee would provide investment advice to the fund and distribute the fund's shares. It might also provide Federal's insurance companies with a vehicle for customers settling insurance claims to reinvest their proceeds at a competitive rate. In addition, we could lighten our customer credit card receivable burden by offering a debit card tied to a customer's money-market account, encouraging more cash purchases in our stores."

I then turned to Lawrence and John. "What are your thoughts, and what has your work uncovered?"

John agreed with me and presented some of the technical details and requirements for structuring the deal, including a contract with an investment adviser and underwriter, registration with the SEC, and licensing of personnel.

After listening to the morass of legal technicalities, I addressed Lawrence directly. "What is in this for Federal, and how does it realize a benefit from offering its customers this type of product without becoming overwhelmed with regulation for what is a secondary or tertiary source of business?"

"Regarding your first question," he said, "I think you have adequately presented Federal's reasons for getting into this business, and I assume the accountants and underwriters will look at the projected revenues and trends and cost of implementation and all those things they do. With respect to the regulatory question, I have a bit of concern. Right now the FTC regulates you, and there's the SEC as a publicly traded company and some international trade-agency regulations. The difference between how you are regulated now versus regulation under the SEC as a broker dealer is like the little leagues and the majors. My opinion is that we create a wall between these two businesses to make everyone's life bearable. We can structure this in a way to avoid some of the initial hurdles and navigate the minefields so that this makes sense coming out of the gate, but the future is going to require some heads-up self-regulation and internal vigilance. In my opinion, this needs to operate through veiled subsidiaries. I see a contract with a licensed investment adviser.

"Also, I don't see Federal registering as a broker but contracting with a broker dealer for the sale and distribution of the funds' shares. Notwithstanding this, if Federal is in any way involved in influencing the purchasing of the funds' shares, they may be required to register as a broker. We will have to look into this further as we gain more information about the nature of Federal's activities. I can go on, but I think it's better if I do some more work and get our legal memorandum and report to you next week or so. At that point, we should be ready to go before Federal's board. How does that fit with your schedule?"

"That sounds great," I said. "The board meets several weeks from this Friday. I appreciate the work you guys are doing and look forward to seeing your report." I gathered my things to leave. "One last thing. Will you consider in your analysis the impact of this deal on Federal's existing as well as future business plans? I'm concerned that with all that Federal has its hands in, there are bound to be potential conflicts out there."

"Yes, of course. We have either suggested or managed most of the acquisitions, mergers, and other affairs of Federal and will lay this project against the others to be sure it doesn't negatively impact outcomes. I will speak to the head of financial services to get his take on this project," Lawrence said.

After shaking hands with Lawrence and John, I proceeded to exit the conference room and headed down the corridor to the reception area.

I was feeling good about the meeting and proud of myself. It was an endorphin high, similar to that of an athlete who surpasses his expectations in a game, and my adrenaline was flowing. Feeling pumped, I thought about the attractive receptionist I encountered earlier. Not wanting to be obvious, I contemplated what to say to her on my way out: "How are you? Working hard? What are you doing later? What's your sign?" Stupid things that just didn't cut it.

As I entered the reception area, the girl with the amazing eyes and blond hair looked up, and our eyes met and lingered for more than a moment. Before I could think of something appropriate and charming to say, she said, "Finished, Mr. Baros? Hope you had a productive meeting."

"Wow, she remembered my name," I thought.

"Yes, we had a good session, but plenty of work to do. And your name is?" I said.

"Katrina."

"Katrina—interesting name. Is that Russian?"

"Yes, my grandfather immigrated here years ago."

"Well, lucky for Winthrop & Hudson."

"Well, thank you. That is kind of you," she said, with a broad smile that revealed a full mouth of straight, pearly white teeth.

Before I could say anything more, a tall, well-dressed, tanned man with a full head of mixed-gray hair entered from the spiral staircase. Katrina quickly turned her attention away from me to address him.

"Mr. Guillermo, you are scheduled to attend the Management Committee meeting with Mr. Whitman at four thirty. I left a message with your secretary."

"*¿Donde esta el lugar?*"

Surprisingly, Katrina responded in Spanish.

I was feeling somewhat awkward and hesitated, trying to decide to stay or resume my exit, seeing that my Katrina was now totally engaged in a linguistic romp with her new beau and feeling left out of the ménage à trois.

Mr. Guillermo finally left, never acknowledging my presence.

"I apologize for that. He is so rude and impolite. Most of these guys are the same, and think I'm supposed to fall over them," Katrina said.

"Sounds like you have issues with him."

"It's just today or yesterday and next week. I just hate the attitudes of some of the men and how they treat the 'help.' Sorry. I didn't mean to say that—not professional at all."

"No need to apologize; we all need to vent the stress. Not to change the subject, but where can a guy get a nice late lunch around here? Any suggestions?"

"Oh, there are plenty of places. What do you want?"

"Just something casual, light. Seafood?"

"Why not go to the Seaport? It's close, and it has plenty of seafood places."

"Oh yes, good suggestion. Care to join me? You seem like you could use a glass of wine."

"That would be delightful, but I can't get out until later. The office is shorthanded, and client meetings are insane today."

"Well, maybe another time. Here's my card. Call me, and we'll have drinks and chat."

"Thank the gods; what was that?" I thought once I got outside. "She was beautiful and seemed interested. Should have gotten her number. Hope she calls. Maybe I'll call her at the work number or see her next time I come back. Who was that guy? Clearly Hispanic but not Puerto Rican or Dominican—probably Spanish or South American. He looked European and white."

CHAPTER FIVE

I t was a pleasantly bright fall day. It was late afternoon, and the streets were filled in lower Manhattan. As far as air quality in New York goes, it was clear and crisp. Walking through the narrow thoroughfares in the financial district, I headed toward the South Street Seaport on the East River, down from the Twin Towers. Those magnificent towers of concrete, glass and steel stood like pillars holding up the New York City sky, similar to the pillars of the famous Greek Temple of Artemis in the ancient city of Ephesus that held the roof to that architectural wonder. The towers were magnificent, bold, confident, and inspiring. Like a king and queen, they sat on their thrones, and all that surrounded the towers occupied their court.

I entered a café on the southern side of Fulton Street that sat alongside the bumpy cobblestone street and other retail boutiques, galleries, and eateries. I had eaten there before and remembered that it served the best apple cobbler with real whipped cream. In the spring and summer months, the Seaport was an attraction for city dwellers as well as tourists. Street performers, including jugglers, magicians, and musicians, would cavort among the tourists and other onlookers, enhancing the sights and sounds of the thriving maritime seaport.

I asked the hostess for a seat. As she led me to the table, I heard someone call, "Jordan, Jordan...what are you doing here?"

It was Stacey Watson, Maria's BFF and hangout buddy. She knew everything about Maria and me, I assumed.

"Hey, Stacey, what's happening?" I asked. The hostess, who had stopped leading, continued to hold the menu and awaited my direction before proceeding.

"You mind if I join you?" I asked.

"Don't you even ask; just sit down. I need to talk to you, anyway. I was going to call."

"Uh-oh," I thought. I quickly turned toward the hostess and extended my hand to receive the menu. "I'll sit here."

"I'll have the waitress bring you a setting," the hostess said.

"Thank you."

Seated with Stacey was a strikingly attractive mocha-brown woman in business attire with a small face, full, angelic eyes, a sharp chin, and shoulder-length, chestnut-brown hair. Stacey introduced her girlfriend as Nia and explained she was originally from Chicago and had received her master's degree in journalism from Columbia. She was now working for Channel 9 WOR TV station. I sat in the seat next to her, across from Stacey.

Before we had a chance to talk, Stacey's friend apologized for having to leave to finish a presentation on an important community-affairs piece she was preparing for a taping to be aired later in the month. The ladies had finished their meal; Stacey still had a partially filled drink.

"I'll leave a twenty, Stacey...you let me know if I owe you," the media woman said. "Call me. I've got to run. It was nice meeting you, Jordan. Next time we'll have to spend more time. See you guys." And she left.

"Bye, hon. I'll call." Stacey said. I nodded my head and got a full view of her now that she was standing—and was impressed.

"She's such a sweetheart. Too bad she had to leave; you would have enjoyed her conversation…but maybe it's better. This gives us a chance to talk in private," Stacey said.

"Well, I'm surprised to see you here. I haven't seen you since we went out together clubbing, and that had to be two months ago. How have you been? Maria keeps me up to date," I said.

"So, I guess she told you Frank and I aren't together."

"Yeah, she said you were upset. I heard you two went out to drown your sorrows after the breakup."

"I don't know how I got home that night. Last thing I remember is getting in a cab and the driver saying, 'Miss, we're here.' Thank God Maria went home with me that night; I would have never made it. Probably would have ended up in Central Park or a shelter."

"I liked Frank; he was a nice guy."

"Frank was out for Frank. He didn't even give me the courtesy of his intentions to move to Atlanta until after he had packed his bags and was on his way to the airport. That bastard had the nerve to say, 'I'll call after I get settled.' I was with him for three years. Three years of blood, sweat, and tears, and all I get is 'I'll call you'!"

"Maria said he was leading you on with plans for the future, including buying some property and getting engaged."

"Yes, we went through that cycle, and I should have known it was all talk. Whenever I gave that fool my kitty-kat, he'd start his, 'Baby, I love you and don't want anyone but you. I will give you the world.' The most confused nigga I ever met. Most of them beg like a baby before they get it; this one was just the opposite. That's why I thought, 'Oh, man, this is different. Maybe this will work out.' But enough of him…I got another honey who I'm punishing because of Frank and ain't giving him a thang until I decide it's time…and he's treating me like a queen. I'm going to play this out as long as I can."

"You go, girl…So what else is new? How's the job?"

"That's going well. I love my boss; she's a really cool white girl. We are personal as well as business, and you know, I got the gift of gab, so selling drugs—excuse me, pharmaceuticals—to these white doctors is a piece of cake for me. Talking about cake, I got to watch myself. I go out to dinner…almost…at least three to four times a week at the company expense with clients of mine, 'cause these doctors don't have time during the day to see reps, and you know how these white men are—if they can hang out with an attractive black chick with class, they are living one of their fantasies. And I play it to the hilt; they are the center of my attention. While we are out, nothin's too good for my docs, and you know me—I recommend classy, expensive restaurants with five stars, like Le Cirque, Club Twenty-One, or the Russian Tea Room. And you know where they want me to take them…it's black restaurants and clubs like Sweetwater's, Shark Bar, Sylvia's, and Perks up in Harlem. Not that I have anything against those places; I go there all the time. But for them, it's the novelty of being around blacks. Ironically, that's when I get my best sales and establish the best relationships. They just love being around black folks so they can go back and tell their Long Island golf buddies and Hampton crowd how cool they are, hangin' out at this black club or that one. Anyway, it must be working; I was the company's highest-selling rep this past year, got a free trip to Bermuda…all expenses paid…and those commission checks don't hurt, either. That's another thing…I took that good-for-nothing Frank on a free trip to Bermuda. After all my hard work and I'm supposed to sit by the phone and wait for his call. He can kiss my plump, mildly enlarged, but tight gluteus maximus. I'm sorry, Jordan. I don't mean to act like this."

"Don't apologize to me; I'm enjoying your rant against men. You make me laugh. You need to see Ntozake Shange's play *for colored girls who have considered suicide/when the rainbow is enuf.* She paints black men as the scourge of the earth. I walked out of the play mad as hell."

"Well, I'm glad someone finds my life amusing…someone else told me to check out her play. Shit, I could have written the damn thing myself…but forget that. Let's talk about you and my girl."

"Okay, let's talk."

"Jordan, you know I can be direct at times, but my heart is in the right place. The Japanese refer to it as the person with the 'good heart.' It's an admired quality in their society, and I think I am such a person."

"I don't question that; I think you are a good person. I only hope you don't let these ne'er-do-wells take advantage of you," I said with all seriousness, having detected Stacey's change in mood.

"That can be a problem, but trust me—I'm growing to be as deceitful and calculating as the rest of the trash out here. Seriously, Jordan, I'm concerned 'bout Maria and you."

I sat up, attentive, and wondered where Stacey was going with this. About this time, the waitress came over and took my order of a crab cake appetizer and Bombay gin and tonic with a splash of grapefruit. Stacey ordered another Stoli, chilled with two olives, and continued talking after the waitress left.

"This relationship is taking a lot out of Maria, and I don't like what I'm seeing. Last week I spoke to Sharon Williams, a friend of ours… mostly mine—Maria doesn't have many female friends of her own. About Maria's birthday…Sharon is having something at her place in two weeks and suggested that we combine it with a little celebration for Maria. Sharon's good hearted like that, and besides, she likes Maria. We were talking about maybe making it a surprise, but I dismissed that idea when I realized you wouldn't be able to come. Why give a surprise when the main person in her life might not be there?"

"I hear what you're saying, but I don't think my being there or not should prevent you and her friends from celebrating or showing your love. It's difficult for all of us; I can't even begin to share with you the whole situation."

"I understand. I can imagine all you must be going through."

"It's a difficult situation. There is no positive outcome. I never planned things to go the way they have, with Andre, her ex-lover, her moving to Brooklyn. I always found her attractive, but we started as friends." I paused, sipping my drink.

"Your girl—and I love her—is in such a way that I hate to go out with her lately, and you know she and I have been hanging out for years doing the Manhattan thing. We know each other so well, we can read the other's mind. If I'm out and some guy tries to hit on me who I *don't* want to be bothered with, Maria will pick that up in a minute and find a way to rescue me without shattering the jerk's ego. Well, let me rephrase that—most of the time."

"I know. I've seen you two in operation, and the excuses, the 'Let's go to the ladies' room' act, never to return to the original spot—you don't think that's insulting?"

"Well, some of them deserve it. Where does a gap-toothed, unemployed, sagging dude get the audacity to think he can get with all this?" Stacey said, using her hands to create an hourglass figure, laughing as she spoke.

"You're rough, girl."

"We went to a party in Queens last weekend, and there was this guy...I swear...who looked exactly like you. He and his brother were the best-looking guys there, and they were checking Maria out. And I told her so. In the past, my girl would have been right on it, but she paid no attention to them and spent most of the evening sitting in a chair looking bored or talking to the girls."

"Yeah, she told me about that and said she didn't have a good time. She said she wasn't feeling well."

"Yeah, lovesick 'cause you weren't there," Stacey half joked. "But I really wish you could come to the party and help celebrate her birthday."

"We'll see...when is it and where...again?"

"My girlfriend Sharon's place in Harlem, three weeks from this Saturday. I'll get you the exact address," Stacey said.

"I don't know her and don't recall Maria mentioning her."

"She has a beautiful brownstone in Harlem. She's a gynecologist, and her husband's in the music business with PolyGram, so there should be some celebs or celeb wannabes and good food and music. Plus, she used to go out with this young filmmaker before she got married. He's from California, went to film school on the West Coast, young looking, skinny...not that soft on the eyes, but he's supposed to be brilliant and just starting out. He has a movie coming out soon. I think you'd enjoy meeting him. You're like a cool nerd—no offense. Personally, I think that is the best type."

"No offense taken—plus, all I heard was *cool*."

I had received my crab cakes and salad by now and asked Stacey if she wanted to taste some.

Without hesitating, she said, "Sure." She took a forkful and put it to her mouth. "That is delicious, just like the ones in Maryland—more crab than filling!" Stacey exclaimed.

"Glad you enjoyed it." I said, emphasizing *enjoyed* because I was not inclined to share any more.

"It's good to see you, Stacey. You are still as crazy as ever, but it's a good crazy. Don't change."

"Well, no one has ever accused me of being boring, and if they do, they must have issues."

"I hear that. I was hoping to come here and chill with a drink and crab cakes. I just left this meeting. I'm creating this new financial-services product for my company's customers and dealing with those pompous corporate lawyers. My main concern is that if anything goes wrong, I know I'll be the goat."

"Why do you think something will go wrong?"

"I hope everything goes smoothly, and I'm checking and re-checking things as the deal develops, but you never feel secure.

I'm not connected, the politics are greater than me as an individual, and bottom line, I'm a black man in a sea of white, without a lifeline."

"I hear you and admire your courage. I also feel the same way, but I think it's different for black men than women. We are not as threatening. I guess it's the sexism and being black. White men always controlled women, white or black, and in turn feel less threatened by us than by you men. I think they are physically threatened by black men," Stacey said.

"Yeah, they fucked the black women, but hung and castrated the men. So the violation difference is rape versus murder and mutilation. Enough of that," I said, having finished my food and drink. "I'll see what I can do about the party; I need to check on some things. Also, if you need me to help out...money, running around, or whatever, let me know, okay?"

"Oh, sure, and what I said is not to pressure you into coming or not. I don't know your wife and don't wish to get involved with your marriage except that I'm Maria's friend, and she confides in me because I'm her friend. And I see things through her. I have been with her through thick and thin. You know what I mean?"

"I know you're looking out for your friend, and I understand that. Everything is just more complicated than just any one person," I said and then quickly added, "I've got to run, Stacey. I need to get uptown and catch a train home."

I asked the waitress for the bill and paid my bill as well as Stacey and her friend's prior bill.

Stacey thanked me. "I'm supposed to meet my friend later at a club in Chelsea. I need to get to a phone to call him and get the address. And by the way, Maria says you have a good connection for the party delicacies. Can you set me up with your man?"

"No problem. I'll get back to you. You want to share a cab?"

"You go ahead; I don't want to hold you up. I'll go inside and make a call and then catch a cab or take the subway later."

"You sure?"

"Yes, go ahead. I don't think I'm meeting him until seven, and it's only five now. I'll do some shopping and then head uptown later. Give me a hug."

I hugged Stacey and kissed her on the cheek before departing to flag down a cab. "Damn, didn't get my apple cobbler," I thought, as I settled into the cab and raced through lower Manhattan, headed to midtown's Penn Station after a full day.

CHAPTER SIX

It had been a week since Trina left the hospital. She was feeling a lot better considering, but we had avoided further discussion about our marital situation, her mental state, and our dissatisfactions. We knew communication was essential, but neither of us took the initiative to open up, and so much was happening, it was easy to avoid the discomfort of talking about more bad stuff. It was an unnatural avoidance.

One day, I guess Trina finally felt she had the energy and called me at work. "I need for us to talk and would like to go out away from the house and bedroom to do it. I have a lot that needs to be said."

"Sure, I've been thinking about that myself."

"What time can you be home?"

I thought about my schedule. "I should be there by seven thirty at the latest. Where do you want to go? Is Leonia's Restaurant okay?"

"No, not there…unless you want the whole town listening to us. Somewhere quiet and anonymous…you think of somewhere. I'll see you when you get here." And with that, Trina hung up.

I arrived home around seven as I had promised and suggested that we go to a quaint Italian restaurant in one of the neighboring towns, known for good food as well as celebrity Mafia clientele and local politicians.

⚊⧓⧓⚊

We took a corner table; I sat facing the entrance, with Trina on the opposite side facing me. After we settled in, the waiter asked in a heavy Italian accent, "What may I get the beautiful lady and handsome young man to drink?"

Trina turned to me. "What are you having?"

I responded by asking if she wanted wine, but she instead placed her order for an Absolut martini, chilled with three olives.

I was somewhat surprised because this was not a drink Trina normally ordered. "Well, I guess that answers my question," I said and ordered a gin and tonic. The waiter asked if I preferred a particular gin; I said, "Bombay."

After the waiter left, Trina looked me directly in the eyes. "I needed something strong tonight; hopefully, I can drink with the medication. Who cares? You'll take me home, won't you?"

"Of course," I said. "Who's been taking you home all these years?" I recalled an incident when Trina and I were first dating, and we both got drunk at a party and ended up sleeping in the car—me in the front and her in the back.

Trina smiled. "At least we knew we couldn't drive. Those are moments when I felt you loved me. You were so concerned and protective then…what happened, and when did it happen?"

Before I could respond, the waiter returned with the drinks and presented the evening specials that included a Dover sole over sautéed spinach surrounded by white cannellini beans, which I ordered. Trina ordered a seafood almandine, which was served over capellini. We agreed to share a calamari appetizer. I didn't answer Trina's question. We both sat for a brief moment saying nothing, sipping on our drinks, and dipping the warm Italian bread in the olive oil and parmesan mixture the waiter had prepared for us.

Trina broke the silence. "I thought of writing you a letter. So much has gone on, and for too long we have not talked about the many things in our lives the past few years. I find it easier to talk to you on the phone or through a letter."

"Why is that?" I asked.

"I don't know." Trina furrowed her brow and wrinkled her nose like a rabbit. "Maybe because I can continue without being interrupted, reflect, and gather my thoughts. You know how volatile you can be."

"So you want me to be quiet and not interrupt? That's gonna be hard."

"You know what I mean. Your intensity brings out a reaction in me, and I get choked up...cry, can't think, and then you say I'm being irrational." She paused. "Anywayyy...well, I've been home with the boys for the past eight years."

"Yes," I said, nodding.

"I was able to spend a lot of time with them—first Chad and then Jared. They would get off that kiddie school bus with their little papers and arts and crafts...so proud of their accomplishments in school, and I could enjoy the moment with them...real time. And I watched both develop from infants, changing and growing day to day. It's been an amazing time. That was such a pleasant, rewarding period. But with all that, I still haven't felt fulfilled. We have struggled at times as your career has developed, the bills... we need to buy a larger house. I feel I should go back to work and help out with the expenses. I'm anxious to get back to my career...it seems our friends are enjoying a better lifestyle than us. I want more for us, as much as we deserve. Until recently you worked two jobs, teaching at night and spending so much time away from home. I'm lonely and feeling unappreciated. Do you understand what I'm saying?"

Just as Trina finished her thought, the waiter appeared with our appetizer and placed the calamari and marinara sauce between us, giving each of us a small plate. The waiter looked at me and asked graciously, "Is everything all right? Anything else I can get you for now?"

"No, everything is fine. Thank you," I said.

"Your meal will be out shortly. Bon appetit." With that, he left.

I put some of the calamari on my plate and added a little of the sauce. "So you enjoyed being a housewife and stay-at-home mother somewhat?"

"Yes, I enjoyed it for the most part. But my point is, now what? The boys are older, independent. I want to go back to work, pursue my career, find myself again. Then I become afraid...what's going to happen to us? You come home late during the week and spend at least one day or evening out on the weekends. I don't understand. Maybe I haven't done the best job of balancing husband, family, and personal ambition. I don't know how your insides feel, but mine feel as if they are being ripped apart. These last several years have been torture; I'm completely drained...weak and always sick! If things don't change, I could have a breakdown."

I was listening intently and knew exactly what Trina was saying. I could not argue against the deceit that I had internalized the past year. There was no way I could deny the personal destruction my actions were causing.

"Do you know that this is the first time in years we have talked like this...about our relationship?" I said. "Our communication recently has been about money, kids, my jobs, and the house—everything but us."

"Whose fault is that?" Trina asked, her voice rising. "You don't express your emotions except when you are angry. What about love? That's an emotion, too! You never allow me to be very close; you are distant, even after all these years. I may go to my grave never really knowing who you are. Let me in and share not just your conscious thoughts...share the deeper thoughts, even if painful and dark. This will allow us to grow together, break the barriers that prevent intimacy. This is a painful and difficult time for both of us."

The conversation was so intense that Trina acted startled when the waiter told her to watch herself because the plate was hot. She then sat back in her seat as he placed the capellini with seafood in front of her. He then did the same with my Dover sole. The combination of aromas and heat escaping from the dishes momentarily anesthetized us.

"Can I refresh your drinks?" the waiter asked.

Trina's drink was half-empty, but I ordered another for myself. The sparse restaurant clientele that evening lent privacy to our conversation.

"This looks good. You want some?" I asked.

"I'll have some. You want to taste mine?"

"Yeah, it smells good."

We helped each other sample the entrées. The waiter returned with my drink and then stepped away to allow his guests to enjoy dinner, keeping a watchful eye from a distance should we need his services.

"Ummmh, so good," Trina said.

"Yep, the fish is fresh. That's why I like this place; they must go to the fish market every morning and pick out the specials. It tastes like they just caught it."

"Where was I?" Trina said.

"You were saying I don't express my feelings, and the void it causes leaves you anxious. I don't completely agree because I have said to you for some time that we are boring each other to death. I need the same as you—affection, gratitude…intimacy. With you, the predictable patterns make me feel our relationship is as business partners with objectives, goals, and plans. It's a job. And the last years, you haven't been yourself…I miss the old Trina."

Trina had stopped eating once I began and was now looking up, ready to respond.

"How do you expect someone to feel good about themselves and be sexy and loving when there's no encouragement or compliments from her husband? But let's not go there. Let's not argue and accuse. Let's try to uncover the source of our problems and try to come up with some answers."

"Okay, I agree. I'll shut up."

"You don't have to shut up; just let me say what I have to say. You have not always been like this. The reason I found you so interesting was your expressiveness. You talked about your vulnerability… you called it your 'sense of inadequacy,' never being good enough, and how I was such an encouragement because I believed in you. I encouraged you to not accept less than your potential. We filled out applications for you to go to law school. I'm committed. I never thought of you as inadequate…only strong, capable, insightful, and focused. But now I don't know. Maybe you are inadequate, weak, self-centered. Can you be there for me the way I have been for you? Your personality is a mess, and it seems like your feelings are buried under layers of scar tissue. You're afraid to let them surface…even to your wife. What are you afraid of?"

"What do you mean? I'm not afraid," I said.

"Who do you show your other side to? The kids? You have no real close friends," she said and then quickly made an apology. "I didn't mean that. I apologize; I didn't intend to be the wife bitch tonight."

This remark was a jab to the heart. "That's a relief. It's not true. People like me, and I like people. Yes, I am quiet, mostly introspective. I like my space and the solitude and comfort it brings."

"Oh…is that where you are when you are out so much—solitude…quiet? Or is it another woman?"

"What are you saying? I'm working. We have kids, bills, and responsibilities that require me to be the CEO, lawyer, psychologist, financial planner, decision maker, and everything else." I never addressed the question about another woman.

I felt Trina's pain and contemplated confessing my indiscretions but decided not to. The idea that another woman was the recipient of my romantic urges was unsettling. Trina was the mother of my kids…the love and fidelity she gave was complete. All things considered, I loved what Trina and I had.

Trina regained her composure, twirled the pasta and seafood on a fork, and lifted a spoonful to her mouth. She frowned as if to say, "What had tasted delightfully exquisite earlier is completely tasteless now."

"I also feel inadequate and vulnerable, and I know I retreat into myself for comfort. I feel so alone. Even more so now…these are the times you realize you're in the world all by yourself, and it shouldn't be that way. I have no true girlfriends I can confide in. I must maintain my image…my so-called friends don't want to hear me but expect me to be sensitive to their problems. You are my best friend, and now even you aren't available. People think for some strange reason that I'm above it all, that what affects most people doesn't affect me. They say I'm smart and strong…and have a loving husband. Well, I don't feel strong and smart right now. I feel as if my life is out of control, just spinning; it's like this weight on my chest as I struggle for air. Then I get angry. Angry at not having a close friend, angry with you and the world for not seeing or listening, not noticing me, the wounds you're inflicting. I'm tired of masking my pain and suffering."

Trina was crying now, and tears were running down her cheeks. She apologized. "I didn't want you to see me cry. Excuse me." She opened her Fendi bag to remove a Kleenex to dry her eyes and wipe the tears from her cheeks.

I didn't know what to say at that point and was also hurting. I had always been her prince, her first and only true love. No matter what happened, she still loved me. For me, this had always been difficult to accept. Love had not come easy in my life. It appeared in different forms. I never knew my father, who left when I was an infant. My relationship with my mother, Rachel, had its own issues. I questioned the bond, warm, maternal love that babies and yes, grown men need. I was close to my grandma; she cared for me as an infant until I was three years old, when my mother remarried. Conflicted bonds a person experiences as a child affect his or her ability to receive and give love. Not knowing what to say, I sat and thought but said nothing.

"Are you ready to leave? Do you want to go home?" I asked.

"I guess. I can't finish this."

I called the waiter over as Trina excused herself to go to the ladies' room. He asked, "Will that be all? Can I get you some dessert, an after-dinner cordial? Or how about an espresso or cappuccino?"

"No, I think that will be it for now. Give my regards to the chef, and please wrap my wife's food to go. Thank you."

After Trina returned, she gathered her things while I paid the bill. We left the restaurant to head home. There was no further conversation during the short ride home. *The Quiet Storm* was on WBLS, and Anita Baker's song "Giving You the Best that I Can" played. When we arrived home, June, our housekeeper, had put the boys to bed. Trina said she was exhausted and headed upstairs.

"Are you coming?" she asked.

"Yes, in a minute," I said.

I sat in the TV room for a moment to capture a brief respite and to reflect on what had happened at dinner before I went upstairs.

When I got upstairs, Trina was still in the bathroom doing her hair and getting ready for bed. I hung my suit up neatly in the closet. Trina had thrown her clothes over the footboard on her side of the bed. I slipped on pajama bottoms with my undershirt and jumped into bed. Trina joined me shortly, got settled on her side, and rolled over to kiss me on the cheek.

"I'm glad we talked tonight. How do you feel?" she asked.

"I'm fine, but we have a lot more to talk about, I think."

"I know...but I feel better right now. Are you going to sleep?" Trina asked.

"No, I'm awake, just thinking about everything."

"You know what is so strange? Right now I want to make love to you. I have this overwhelming need for you to be inside me...is that crazy?" Trina asked.

"No, this has been quite a date, and as masochistic and sadistic as we are...no, it's not crazy." I turned over and ravenously kissed Trina as she began to feverishly remove my pajama bottoms, stroking my member with her hand and aggressively leading me to insert my erection into her. She was moist and ready, thrusting her hips and rubbing her clit directly on my manhood. Before I completely entered her, she switched positions to be on top and then guided me inside her with her hand. She moaned seductively as I alternatively sucked the nipples of her breasts as she leaned forward to put them in my mouth. I continued to love her until we climaxed and eventually fell asleep, arm in arm.

CHAPTER SEVEN

A few days later, I called Maria to confirm our plans for lunch but was caught by surprise when she suggested more than just sandwiches.

"Why don't we go to a hotel and order room service?" she suggested.

Without hesitating, I said, "Sounds good. You must be reading my mind. I'll get a room at the Waltham on Seventh and Fifty-Third and meet you there about twelve thirty. I don't have to be back to work until later; can you get an extended lunch?"

"Yes, I'll see what I can do...and I don't have to be a psychic to read your mind."

"'Cause I always want you? I'll see you around twelve thirty at the Waltham."

I felt excitement just thinking about her, and it was apparent from the bulge in my pants under the desk. I called to get a reservation and tried to get as much done at work as I could before lunchtime.

I promptly arrived at the hotel around twelve-fifteen and checked into a room with a king-sized bed. I called Maria. "Have you left yet?" I joked.

"I'm on my way. Just ended a meeting and kicked everyone out the office," she said.

"I'm in room five-twelve. I'll see you soon."

"Okay, sugar. Bye."

Maria didn't arrive until half an hour later. She was carrying a bag and explained as she got in the room why she was delayed. She had stopped at a bistro and ordered us a picnic lunch.

"You didn't have to do that; I told you we could order something later," I said.

"This is better. I don't want anyone coming up here...and this will give us more time together. I got your favorite—a roast turkey on baguette with cheddar. There's enough for us to share as well as some fresh fruit and a sparkling fruit drink."

The lunch was packed in a nice little wicker basket and tied with a ribbon.

"Nice work, baby. This looks good. Come give me some sweet kisses as an appetizer."

Maria bent down and gave me a juicy, wet kiss on my lips and in her sultry way asked, "Is that all you want?"

She wore a Tahari blue business suit, a cream-colored blouse and matching, cream-colored Christian Louboutin high heels. I had taken off my clothes earlier, including my dark, tan-colored Ralph Lauren gabardine suit jacket and Hugo Boss striped yellow tie, which matched perfectly. I was sitting on the edge of the bed when Maria kissed me. I unbuttoned her suit jacket during the exchange. She moved back to take it off and began to unbutton her blouse.

I continued to undress and quickly moved under the covers without taking my eyes off her, as she was giving a burlesque show

I did not want to miss. Underneath her suit, she wore a beige lace bra with matching lace panties and cream stockings fastened to a garter belt. She removed her bra as I continued to be intrigued by her performance. She crossed her arms over her chest to suggest modesty, did a Marilyn Monroe shimmy and shake, and got into bed, shoes and all.

"Is it all right if I leave my shoes on?" she asked, already knowing what the response would be.

Trying to be controlled, I coolly responded, "So this means I can't lick your toes?"

"That's next time," Maria said. She put her arms around my neck and pulled me down to her open mouth for a deep, wet, prolonged kiss.

This was not the end to the surprises from Maria. The panties she wore were cut out at the crouch to serve a very specific purpose. So without having to remove anything more, I made love to Maria, her stockings, garters, panties, and Christian Louboutins.

I briefly thought about work and wondered how I could return, the way I was feeling. Maria was lying in my arms in a catatonic state for the moment, looking radiant. Other things were slowly beginning to enter my mind. Originally I had a specific purpose for seeing Maria that day: I wanted to tell her about things with Trina and also wanted to see what I could do for her upcoming birthday, but I needed to be cautious not to mention the semisecret party Stacey was planning. I dared not have such a conversation before making love. I did not want to jeopardize the mood but now felt compelled to talk.

"A lot has happened since we had dinner last week."

"Yes," Maria said, as if in a drugged stupor. "What about it?"

"A few nights ago, Trina and I went to dinner. She's had a lot on her mind, and things haven't been right for a while. Women have these instincts, you know."

"Yeah. Is this what you were talkin' about the other day on the phone...you had something to tell me?" Maria said, showing a little more life than she had moments earlier.

"Well, she started to question me about our marriage, my love, and if I was seeing someone. For a minute, I wanted to tell her the truth, but I didn't."

"So what did you say?" Maria had perked up now.

"We talked and agreed things were not right. She is mad, hurt... feels self-conscious about her looks and me. She wants to go back to work. She said she would try to be more focused on our marriage, but the kids...her staying at home...everything has taken its toll over the past few years."

"Oh my God! What are you going to do?" Maria asked. "They all say they'll change when they are threatened but go back to the same ways later."

"I don't know what I'm doing or going to do. Haven't really thought about it. Got this work project that is killing me. Can't handle everything right now. The kids, Trina, you, the job."

"How is your sister? Have you seen her lately?" Maria asked.

"My sister? Why do you ask?" It seemed like a non sequitur.

"I just know how you confide in her and was wondering if she knows about us."

"No. I haven't talked to anyone, certainly not my sister, about this. I talk to her but wouldn't go there with this. Plus, she and Trina are close; I don't want to put her in such an awkward situation. I can't explain to myself what's happening. Things are just crazy now. I wasn't goin' to tell you because I don't know where this is headed."

Maria put the palm of her right hand on my left cheek, guided me forward, and gave me a delicate kiss. "You know I'm here for you and love you."

"I know, baby. It's just a bad time, and I have to let you know about things. Are you sure this is what you want?"

"Is it what you want?"

"What time is it?" I asked without answering the question, feeling that enough had been said, simultaneously looking at my Movado watch on the nightstand. "It's almost two-thirty...we've got to get out of here."

"Oh shit! I have a meeting at three I need to be at!" Maria shouted. She gathered her clothes and raced into the bathroom.

I sat for moment, gathered my things, and barged into the bathroom with Maria, who had taken a shower and was now applying her makeup. Amazingly, Maria finished in a flash and yelled back to me while I was still in the bathroom, "I'll call you later. Kisses, baby. I gotta go."

Maria's office was just right around the corner.

"Okay, babe. I'll call you. What's happening this weekend?" I asked.

"Nothing, probably seeing *mi madre*...why?"

"We'll talk. Bye and thanks," I stammered.

"Thanks for what? I gotta run. See ya."

I came out of the shower and saw the picnic basket sitting on the dresser. I unwrapped the turkey sandwich with the intent of taking a bite and ended up eating the whole thing and drinking the fruit juice. "Damn, that was good. I was hungry," I thought. I've been told that with a few exceptions—some monkeys—dolphins and humans are the only mammals that engage in sex for pleasure. When this life is over I want to come back as a dolphin. I checked the room to make sure we hadn't left anything behind and left to go back to the office.

CHAPTER EIGHT

I received a call last night from my sister, Wanda. She said, "I don't want to get into it now, but can we meet after work tomorrow? It's important that we talk."

I had no idea what she was talking about and didn't speculate. From her voice inflection, it sounded urgent. I said okay, and we decided to meet at a familiar restaurant. My sister lives in a neighboring town.

After work, I drove from the train station to the restaurant, still wondering what Wanda wanted to talk about. The place is a privately owned pizza shop and local bar that lacks the trendiness of franchised establishments. The mixed clientele and reputation for good pizza and drinks has sustained the place for decades. It was a weekday, so the patronage was sparse, with a few sports enthusiasts sitting at the bar, watching the pregame show of a baseball game. We took a booth away from the bar that gave us a fair degree of privacy. I hugged Wanda and kissed her on the cheek. We ordered pie and a pitcher of beer.

"Thanks for coming out. I'm sorry for being so secretive, but I've been thinking about this and trying to decide how to approach you," Wanda said.

"Okay," I said, hoping we could finally end the suspense.

"Jordan, I'm so disappointed in you. You have a good wife, and you are going to mess it up and live your life as a lonely, heartbroken man. You need to wake up and stop what you are doing."

I was shocked at the bluntness and was completely surprised. What did she know, and how did she know it?

Wanda explained the source of her knowledge as six degrees of separation. "Do you know a girl named Stacey Watson?"

"Yeah, I know Stacey."

"Well, recently you had lunch with her and my girlfriend, Nia. We went to school together, and she works in broadcast, like me. It's a small world."

Now things became clearer. I remembered the attractive woman, if not her name, who left in a hurry to return to work.

"Your friend, Stacey, has shared all your secrets with Nia, and it wasn't difficult for her to put two and two together. Once she realized you were my brother, she tried to cover it up, but I know everything. The girl you are seeing has a reputation. She is going to use you like the others."

I sat stunned and silent.

"I've been thinking about your problems over and over again, and there's a lot I don't understand. I try to be objective. I know you have demands—you work two jobs, commute every day to New York, and take on your family responsibilities and bills. And nothing is one-sided...Trina has not been looking her best lately. She tells me she wants to go back to work, pursue her career. You two shouldn't lose sight of what you have. Talk, talk, talk. Trina is a fabulous woman. And she certainly is no dummy. If you thought she lost some of her pizzazz, why didn't you just tell her? It's there. She may have just needed you to remind her."

At this point, I was speechless. I tried to gather myself. I apologized for my actions and expressed appreciation for Wanda's concern.

"So much is happening, and much is surreal. You have laid it on the table, and I feel bad. This is not a role I am accustomed to, as your big brother."

"Do you mean being caught or cheating?" Wanda asked.

"Look, I'm embarrassed that you know. I've been a deceitful liar. I don't feel good about that. I've deceived myself and other people to maintain this affair. But step back for a minute. You remember your situation a few years ago when you asked me for help?"

"What? The thing with Rodney?"

"Yes, you know what I'm talkin' 'bout. You confided in me about someone you were going out with and how difficult that relationship was for you. You ended up in counseling. You, of all people, should empathize with me and this thing I'm going through."

"Yes, I was in love, and it was wrong, and it hurt. I hurt myself, but I was single and learned a hard lesson."

"What do you think Rodney's wife would say about you if she knew you were fucking her husband for two years? Your actions were not victimless. I felt your pain. A family was damaged, and you are still scarred. Trust me—I don't bring this up to condone what I've done; I'm just saying this is an equivalent, so you may better understand how I'm feeling. I was more concerned about you as opposed to your actions. I was always there for you to talk to without judgment and blame."

"Look, my brother, I hear you, and I don't want to judge, but I love you guys—Trina and my nephews—dearly. I want the best for them, for everybody. But ultimately it lies with you. No one can make you cheat. You wanted to. We all have a flirtation—that's natural—but this is tacky. What about her and the kids? Come on, think about Chad and Jared. I expect you to clean this mess up. If you don't tell Trina the truth, I will. You can believe that. You've got one hell of a cleanup job ahead of you. I hope for your sake you can work it out, or else you may end up one lonely old man. Please work hard to put it all back together again. Even if you and Trina can't work things out, you've got to get your head straight!"

I responded with mixed anger, defensiveness, and annoyance. "I hear you, but don't threaten me or take this too far. I will handle things; you have no right to go beyond this conversation. You curse me out without hesitation and have already passed judgment. Understand what I'm going through. I'm disappointed in a lot of things, and I'm sorry if I haven't lived up to everyone's expectations of me."

"I mean everything I just said to you. I do apologize for not beginning with 'I love you, even though you are acting like an asshole!'"

"What kinda backhanded love is this?"

"That's all you get now," Wanda shot back.

Our exchange ended, but before we left, Wanda asked if I had seen our mother recently and made me promise to go see her. I assured her I would. She suggested that I get some time to myself, remove some of the pressure so I could think straight, stay away from Maria, keep my pants zipped, and allow my other head to think about the future. The only thing she left out was "Cure world hunger and eradicate disease."

I sat in my car for a minute before driving home. I understood exactly what Wanda was saying because I said the same things to myself with each transgression. I knew the right thing to do. My values were affected by what others thought of me, and I tried to act accordingly. But my dilemma was this: How did I reconcile doing the right thing with the impulses that were controlling my behavior?

I arrived home a short time later. Trina was upstairs, and the boys were in the TV room playing with a new Transformer toy.

They were so engrossed that they didn't hear me when I entered the room.

"How's my Tuney Bop and Dukey Dukes?" I asked, using my cartoonish nicknames for the boys or "jewels," as Trina liked to say. Both smiled that little-boy smile that touches your innocence and gives your life value as they momentarily draw you into their unblemished innocence.

I bent down to be on their level and asked Chad, the older son, "Who's this?"

Chad's answer was immediate. "Transic."

"This is Machine Man," Jared offered, shoving his toy at me.

"Oh, man, these guys look powerful. Can they fly?" I asked.

"Yes," Chad said and began unfolding layers that looked like legs or arms but converted to wings and engines to make the thing half-human, half-machine.

I went upstairs to change and see Trina before we sat down as a family for dinner.

CHAPTER NINE

I arrived at work early the next day. I didn't feel as bad as I thought I would. I had slept only about four hours. I was mentally alert, but my nerves were raw and exposed. My emotions were affecting me physically. I had lost a considerable amount of weight in the past few months, and it was apparent, given the bagginess of my suits, that I needed to notch another hole in my belt this morning. How long my alertness would last was another question. My mind continued to revisit the conversation with Wanda. The phone rang around nine-fifteen; it was Maria.

"Just wanted to say good morning. How are you?"

"Fine. Nothing a coffee and cinnamon donut can't cure. Didn't sleep well last night."

"Oh, why? How late?"

"Probably didn't get to sleep until two something. I'll feel it later." I avoided any detail and couldn't stomach a replay.

"So, anything you want to tell me, like you don't want to see me anymore, or you need your space...or something like that?" Maria did this line of questioning on occasion, I assumed more for reaction, 'cause I knew she was confident that was not what I wanted.

"No, baby, why would you say that? What are you doing…testing me? You know how I feel 'bout you. I just have a lot on my mind."

Maria half apologized. "I didn't mean to start your day off with all these questions. I just wanted to let you know I miss you and want you to be happy. The main reason I called was to let you know I'll definitely be in Jersey this weekend at my sister Jania's place. I have to take Mom for chemo and will probably stay over until Sunday."

"That's good," I thought and wondered how I could arrange some time with her.

"Chad has a basketball game Saturday morning. What time is your mother's appointment?"

"Early, I think. I'll have to check."

"We'll try to do something Saturday afternoon. It might be a good time to go look for your coat and to see if you can set up an appointment at that place you spoke of. Or if not, we'll have a drink, take a ride…something. We'll talk by Friday and figure everything out," I said.

"Be strong, my love. We'll talk later. I love you."

Marie rarely says "I love you." We both deliberately avoid that, given all the complications of our just being together. This was twice in the past twenty-four hours. I hesitated before responding. "I'm fine; we'll talk Friday about this weekend. Bye."

There was less than two weeks before my big presentation. I needed to organize myself for what was a demanding and important assignment. I had high expectations and knew there would be intense scrutiny of my work. The *Money Fund Report* to the board of directors was due in ten days, and the presentation was due two days later. I needed to completely review the *Winthrop Report*, which had recently arrived and was sitting on my desk. In spite of all I had accomplished professionally, I was still unsure of the next thing. One of the intangible aspects of race is psychological insecurity. Unfairness, real or imagined, was always a part of the equation I had to factor in. I knew that my work product had to be superior. Mistakes that might be overlooked or explained as an aberration for some would be evaluated not just by objective standards but by racial criteria—presumed intellectual inferiority. My grandmother, who was a Brooklyn Dodgers' Jackie Robinson fan, used to say when watching him play, "If you are black, you have to be twice as good."

The *Winthrop Report* was sixty pages long, not including exhibits and other attachments. I had to break it down, make sense of it, revise it in a format for submission to the committee, and raise any questions I anticipated the board to ask. The report was divided into eight sections, from Organizational Requirements to Use of Incentives and Discounts for Customers. This was my first presentation to the board; however, it was not so different from similar presentations I had made before government regulatory authorities, professional bar associations, and juries. Given the significance of this, I considered the analogy of a presentation to the Supreme Court.

I worked late that evening, and it was now close to eight o'clock. I had put in about eleven hours. During my review, I took notes and wrote questions in the margins of the documents. I estimated that with the next few days of uninterrupted effort, I would be reasonably comfortable with the technicalities of the transaction and have the first draft of my report to the board done.

I packed up to head home. I had told Trina I would eat out and decided to get a burger and fries. I needed a break and thought some comfort food would do the trick. I also knew that on the way, I could stop by the Times Square peepshow and see if this sexy girl

I had seen there some time ago was working. Peeps offer the lowest form of intimacy on the sexual food chain, except for dreams and 1-800 sex lines. You enter a booth, drop in a token worth one dollar, and pick up the handset phone device. The curtain opens, and there is a girl on the other side of a Plexiglas shield, who serves up your visual and verbal pleasures for about sixty seconds. The other offering, besides video jerk-off booths, is a circular stage with small, window-like openings that allow you to peer in and touch the women who entertain clients through this twenty-by-twenty-inch opening. It's amazing how much can be accomplished in so tiny an opening. For the man on the go who needs his batteries charged, this is a deal. Getting that endorphin rush with a sexy young woman, some nasty talk, and feeling a titty for a token plus tip is worth it. The popularity is evident, as demonstrated by the traffic that frequents the places.

CHAPTER TEN

Chad had a game at nine thirty Saturday morning, an AAU basketball team for eight-year-olds he played for. I was in the kitchen preparing cereal and juice for his breakfast when he entered.

"Hey, li'l man, you ready?" I said, while extending my hand to him, palm high, for a high five. In his best monosyllabic expression, he replied, "Yeah," while slapping my palm to make a nice, crisp *smack*. We both laughed in admiration of our coordination. I placed my right hand on the back of his head, pulled him into my stomach area, and gave him a huge hug. We had a moment, and everything was great. I stepped back to admire my young charge, dressed in his blue-and-white team colors and matching Air Jordan sneakers. His jersey prominently displayed the number seventeen, the same number I wore when I played basketball.

"Slow down, Chad. Come back here; get your jacket," I told him as we were leaving the house.

Obediently, with a change of expression from "It's time for the Big Game" to "Uh-oh, my bad," he retraced his path and went to get his jacket. Starting all over again with jacket in one hand and water bottle in the other, we headed for the front door. Before we could leave, Trina yelled from upstairs.

"Jared has a birthday party at Games R Us this afternoon, and my mother is taking him there. You said you had to work later, and I have a conference today about new media and will be back around four. Jared will be at my mother's. You can drop Chad off later. I'll pick them up when I get back."

I had plans to meet Maria that afternoon around three.

"I have to do something around three this afternoon. What time is the party?"

"It's two hours, from twelve thirty to two thirty."

"Okay. I'll keep Chad with me and take him to your mother's, okay?"

"Okay. Enjoy. Bye, Chad."

Chad had a good game; his team won. He shared time with the coach's son and usually played two quarters. He was one of the younger kids on the team, and next year he would be a starter. I thought he was ready now but held my tongue and accepted the politics of youth sports. Each parent feels his or her child is more deserving than the next, and all are vicariously living their lives through the kids—*Hoop Dreams* with visions of scholarships and triumphant victories, without the agony of defeat. I was more realistic about sports. Yes, I would have loved to see Chad and Jared go to the next level through their athletic abilities. And subsidized college education would have been a financial blessing. But the odds were not favorable. The odds of a professional sports career are lower than winning the lottery. The prominence of African American athletes can cloud a parent's perspective and encourage thoughts of natural gifts, as if MJ and Magic are the standard as opposed to exceptional individuals with extraordinary gifts. My reason for having my sons participate in team sports was to see them learn that the same qualities required for success in sports are those rewarded in the real world. Conscientiousness, impulse control, teamwork, and a splash of arrogance, which are necessary for success in sports, will serve one well in life. For Trina and me, driving to games and scheduling weekends around the boys' activities were the investment we were willing to make for our young men.

⟨⟩

We left the gym and headed to the car. I encouragingly remarked, "Good game, boy; you were tough out there. Eight points—that was good."

Chad was proud; his eyes glistened and matched the sparkling beads of sweat that dotted his round, cherubic face. "Yep, I could have got more, but the coach keeps taking me out and putting Bruce in. Bruce can't play as good as me. It's just 'cause he's the coach's son."

"Bruce is all right. Plus, he has been playing for two years. Next year, you'll play more; be patient. You need to work on your outside shot and foul shooting. Magic Johnson used to shoot a hundred shots a day when he was your age," I said, not knowing if what I said was true or not. But Magic is his favorite player, so I figured he'd listen to the wisdom in it.

"You want to get something to eat, little man? You must be hungry. You want hot dogs or McDonald's?"

"Can we get hot dogs?" Chad said with the same level of excitement he had demonstrated earlier, in anticipation of his game.

We drove to a greasy Italian hot-dog joint that smelled of Crisco oil–fried potatoes. Peppers and onions leaked through the wax paper and brown-paper bag when the hot dog was packaged to go.

The place was my favorite when I was young. Whenever I was able to hustle some change together, I would reward myself by spending it here. I guess the legacy was passed on, with all the hot dogs I ate; it was probably in my DNA.

After lunch, we headed to the mall to buy the video game I promised Chad. Things had changed so much since I was young. Electronics, digital devices, and entertainment were not around back then. This new phenomenon had recently exploded, with Nintendo replacing Atari in popularity. Chad sat for hours in front of the TV with the joystick, pushing buttons and maneuvering the animated computerized figures on the screen. I remember buying an electric football game for Chad one Christmas, remembering how much I loved it as a kid. One week and three or four games later, it sat in the playroom untouched and was eventually banished to the attic. Another obvious change was kids' dependence on parents for activities like organized sports and playdates. Digitization replaced spontaneity of sandlot games, touch football on a side street, catching lightning bugs in jars, and other pastimes we engaged in as neighborhood kids. I don't recall the last time, if ever, Chad and a group of his friends organized a game of touch football in the backyard or side street or gathered their bats and gloves and went to the park for a sandlot game of baseball. Things had become different, and video games were taking center stage. I wondered at what cost—and not just meaning the price of the games.

We enjoyed our time together, just the two of us. Jared was still too young to hang out, but his time was fast approaching, and I looked forward to it. Sometimes I thought they were giving me more than I gave them. I had the pleasure of reliving and rewriting my childhood through Chad and Jared. The zone allowed a momentary refuge from my personal conflicts. The unconditional mutuality of our love was a life-force.

We drove to Chad's grandmother's house, and Hazel met us at the door. "Hi, Chad," she said and bent down to hug him, imploring him to give her a kiss on her cheek. He hesitated to do it and then responded as asked.

At the same time she was hugging and kissing Chad, she said to me, "What the devil is goin' on with you children? I can't be watching these kids all the time."

I didn't immediately respond but patted Chad on the head and told him to go play with his brother in the family room. Hazel's way of communicating was always negative, and facts were irrelevant. It was the exception, not the norm, that Trina would ask her mother to watch the kids. I realized that she was probably talking about the past month because of the car accident and this weekend's conflicts.

"I'm sorry for this last month; it's been difficult. I guess Trina's told you she's planning to go back to work full time. I have this project keeping me busy, at least for the next few weeks."

"I know you kids are busy. I hope she's makin' the right decision. These boys need their mother; they still young. I pray for you...you need to read the Bible. It talks about all this type of shenanigans and devilishness. That's why these children doing all this bad stuff nowadays." Hazel is a God-fearing Southern Virginia farm girl by heart. Not formally educated—high school at most. When it came to answers, her Bible and God were her references. On the other hand, I'm agnostic, cynical by nature. I let science and facts lead me to the right decision. I can count on one hand the times I attended church this year. Trina attends with the kids more frequently.

I knew nothing good would be gained by continued talk and decided to wrap things up. The best way to do this was to agree with Hazel and promise to do better, even go to church more, telling her what she wanted to hear.

"Let me say good-bye to the boys; I have to go. Trina will be here soon to get them," I said. I went to the family room to say good-bye.

"How ya doin', Jared? How was the party?" I directed my attention to Jared, not having seen him all day.

"It was fun. We rode racing cars and played games."

"That's good. We missed you...the game is for both of you, so make sure you share, Chad, and teach Jared how to play." Not acknowledging anything I had just said, Chad was absorbed in setting up the Nintendo. I repeated myself in a louder voice. "Did you hear me, Chad? Make sure you teach your brother how to play the new game."

"Okay, Daddy, I will," he said.

"Good boy. I've got to go now. See you two later. Mommy will be here soon. When's your next game?"

"I dunno," he said. It was as if he was saying, "Why are you asking me? You're the parent—that's *your* responsibility!"

"I'll check. Bye, boys. Give me a hug."

I left the room and headed to the front door. Hazel was sitting in the living room off the hallway and got up, making her way to the door to let me out.

"I don't know where George is. He said he was going to the store to get a paper, but once he gets down there, he starts talkin' with those folks...and no telling when he'll get back. It takes him one hour to do somethin' that takes five minutes."

"I'm sure he'll be back soon," I said.

"You listen to what I told you, and you will see how God will show the way," Hazel preached as I left to go to my car.

"Yes, ma'am. Tell Trina I will call her later." I was relieved that I was free to go.

CHAPTER ELEVEN

J ania, Maria's older sister, lived in a modest single-family home in suburban New Jersey. A tall, handsome, young man about sixteen or seventeen answered the door when I rang the bell. I introduced myself and asked if Maria was there. The boy said yes but never mentioned who he was. He disappeared up the stairs, calling, "*Titi*, someone here to see you." I knew *titi* was Spanish for *aunt* and guessed that the boy was Jania's son.

I entered the house and stood in the living room. The interior was colorful, if not well coordinated. It had wall-to-wall bluish-green shag carpeting that extended into a dining-room area and a small side room or den to my left. The living room wall was painted in an aqua blue, and the dining area was wallpapered with a green flower print. Straight ahead, against the far wall, was a floor-model entertainment system with a TV and hi-fi stereo-system combination. Above the entertainment console was a prominent, framed picture of a blond Jesus Christ with a religious cross underneath the portrait.

I realized that someone was in the adjacent den and stepped forward to see who was there. I poked my head into the room and saw an older Hispanic woman in a shapeless floral dress sitting in a leather Lazy Boy rocking chair with her head down, reading the Bible. When she looked up from her reading, I took notice of her pale, jaundice-yellow skin tone with prominent brown age spots. She was emaciated and weak looking with thin, gray hair. Her cheekbones and eye sockets were prominently pronounced, giving her a wasting appearance. There was a faint smell of liniment and ointment in the room.

"Hello, Ms. Velez," I said.

Seeming to struggle with a response or trying to determine if she knew me or not, she finally muttered a soft "Hello."

"My name is Jordan; I'm a friend of Maria's," I added.

"My li'l Maria is a good girl. She has to help her mother these days, and I am not as well as I used to be."

"How are you feeling?" I asked.

"Today is not so good, but I am blessed," Carmen answered. "Do you read the Bible, or I guess I should ask what your religion is." Before I could respond, Carmen continued. "It doesn't really matter. I'm Catholic but respect all religions. They all offer a path to living a fulfilling and blissful life. The good books—the Bible, Koran, Torah, and sacred books of the East—are filled with all kinds of common experiences."

"I had a similar talk earlier about religion with someone I know," I said.

"You are young and on a journey. Living things, not spirituality, is what you kids are 'bout. You will have to slow down and discover your soul, your character...the purpose of life." Carmen paused at this moment, reflecting, before she continued.

"I come here in this room every day and spend my time reading and getting in touch with my inner voice. I have spent the bulk of my life giving life to others. Jania and Maria are my people. I fed and cared for my husband. I dedicated my life to others. In turn, I have been blessed and understand what it is to live. I'm a nurturer. And now I'm dying. My body is rotting, but my spirit is stronger than ever."

About this time, Maria entered the room, wearing a pair of Guess jeans and a V-neck, snug-fitting, red Danskin top teasingly showing a little cleavage. She looked at her mother and me and seemed to sense something unusual was happening. She sought to change the mood, realizing that she could not participate in what-ever her mother and I had previously been engaged in.

"*Mama*, you met my friend Jordano. Isn't he adorable?"

"Yes, we had a good talk about you…and he is handsome. Looks like your father's people."

"Hope it was all good, or should I say, 'I know it was good…how sweet I am,'" Maria said.

"I'm a little more humble than Maria, so thank you, ladies, for the compliments. You make me blush," I stated, trying to end the embarrassment I was beginning to feel while still absorbing the earlier conversation I had with Carmen. "You ready to go, babe?" I delicately proposed to Maria.

"Mama, we're going out. You okay? Want me to get you some-thing?" Maria asked.

"I'm fine. You children go. I will sit here with my Bible. Your sister will cook some rice and beans later…I'm fine."

"Madre, *te amo*. I'll be back in a little while," Maria said as she leaned down to kiss her mother and give her a slight hug.

"Good-bye, Ms. Velez. It was a pleasure talking to you. Take care, and feel better," I said as Maria grabbed my hand. We left the room headed to the front door.

"I'm leaving," Maria called out.

"You goin'?" a voice called back, and then a woman appeared at the top of the stairs and leaned over the railing.

"Jania, this is Jordan," Maria said, introducing us.

"Hi," we both responded simultaneously.

"I thought you were staying here," Jania said to Maria.

"No, I told you I was going shopping once Jordan came. I'll be back later."

"Well, nice meeting you, Jordan. Sorry I didn't come down earlier. I'm trying to straighten things up here, and Maria stays in the bathroom, so I can't get nothin' done."

"Shut up, Jania. Jordan doesn't want to hear all that," Maria called back as she opened the front door to go out.

"Nice meeting you, Jania. I'll see you later," I said.

"Nice meeting you. Don't bring her back too soon, so I can get some work done," Jania responded to me.

Determined to have the last word, Maria said, "You know you love me and can't wait for me to come back."

With that, we left to get into my car.

CHAPTER TWELVE

While driving Maria asked, "What were you two talking about? When I walked into the room, you had this intense look on your face."

"Your mother was describing how she felt and her religious beliefs, death, and all. But it was more than just a belief in God; it was how she is making her peace with God through her life experiences. She spoke about her relationship with your father, her nurturing of you and your sister...everything. I was totally unprepared for what she told me. You never talk about your father. What was he like?"

"He died when I was young. I didn't know him that well. We were poor, and he had issues. I try to forget; growing up was not my best time. Mom loved him; he was her only love. She loved him completely and continued her vows even after his death. Unfortunately, I don't think he reciprocated. He was a good provider when he worked, and I'm sure he loved Mom, but family rumor and gossip say he was a womanizer. I may have some brothers and sisters in Pennsylvania, where we lived before he died. I think she knew but gave him a pass, but inwardly she was saddened and hurt. She always said it affected the wholeness of their life together."

Maria stopped at that point and stated, "I don't want to talk about this; it makes me sad."

"I'm sorry. Didn't mean to get this deep. It's just—your mother. Talking to her was interesting."

I was captivated by the unexpected conversation with this wise woman on death's doorstep. Her voice of wisdom had hit a soft spot. I wondered if she knew about Maria and me...my marriage, my cheating? Was she trying to tell me something?

"You know, my mother has been sick awhile; she was given six months to live three years ago. Just recently it has gotten worse. She's also met other cancer patients. She used to go to counseling and assistance sessions and met some interesting people there. A particular woman, originally from Tibet or Nepal, somewhere over there, was a Buddhist, and they became very close. She's had a big influence on her." Maria seemed anxious to continue to talk about her mother.

"Yeah, I was thinking when she was talking that this has got to be a first—a Puerto Rican Buddhist. How was that...her getting to know this woman?"

"Well, the woman—Shrejanee was her name—got Mom to take yoga classes and attend Buddhist retreats and stuff. I began to see a change. Jania and I thought something was wrong and started questioning Mom about this person and all. Mom introduced us to her, and she began to spend more time around the family, and things seemed cool. We got into it a little and started attending yoga classes with Mom and her friend on Saturday mornings. It was all good. I started doing some little chants and trying to focus more on trying to control the things I could and not overreacting to things that I couldn't, which helped bring some peace into my life."

Maria paused briefly and then continued. "But you have to know my mother to really understand all this; my mother has always been the community spiritual healer. She has a remedy for any ill you can imagine. I don't ever remember taking a prescription or something from the drugstore when I was growing up. It was always some home remedy, herb, tea, or root from somewhere. Even now, if you tell her you have this ache or that, she'll know exactly what herbal remedy to prescribe. She was a midwife when we were in Pennsylvania."

"If y'all had been born in the eighteenth century, they would have burned you at the stake for witchcraft," I joked.

"You got that…my grandmother, so I'm told, carried over some mystical things from Puerto Rico. She was into Santeria and used to have séances up in the Heights."

"What is Santa Maria?" I asked.

"S-a-n-t-e-r-i-a. It's an outlawed religious-spiritual cult-like practice that started in Africa and spread to the Caribbean and South America by African slaves. It's similar to Haitian voodoo and all. It can get extreme, with blood sacrifices and all kinds of weird stuff. It's an old backcountry jungle ritual."

"Damn, whatchu talking 'bout, girl? You haven't been practicing any of that Santeria on me."

Maria smiled cunningly and then said, "No, man, I just been puttin' some of this good Latina *chocha* on you."

Before I could react verbally, Maria added, "I must confess to one thing, though. You know how you like apple pie and all? I did put two drops of menstrual blood in the pie I baked for you that time."

"What time? You never baked any pie for me!"

"Calm down, man; I'm just kidding," she said, laughing out loud at my reaction.

"Why are you are messin' with me? What does menstrual blood in apple pie have to do with anything, anyway?"

"You never heard of that? Don't you know? You should know that; it's an ol' black wives' tale. If you do that, you'll keep the man forever; he won't want another woman. Do I have to teach you black history, too?"

"Shuddup, Maria," I said playfully. "That ain't no black history. That's crazy. Menstrual blood in pie…bad shit. Forget that. Don't you do that!"

CHAPTER THIRTEEN

We had on several occasions, either during lunch or after work, looked at fur coats in Bloomingdale's or Saks for Maria. I was willing and wanted to do something special for her. It was going to be her birthday, and I probably wouldn't be able to attend her surprise party, so I was anxious to please. Maria had done her research and asked Stacey and another friend, who recommended a fur boutique in the fashion/garment district in Manhattan that supposedly offered value pricing for designer furs.

We pulled up to the building located on Thirty-Ninth Street between Eighth and Ninth Avenues in the Garment District. It was an unimpressive brick building flanked by other equally unimpressive, warehouse-looking buildings. The only distinguishing feature was a striped green-and-white canopy that extended over the high-gloss, varnished-wood double door with its large brass handles.

"Is this it?" I asked.

"It's the address. I don't see any sign."

"Looks like we can park here. Want a little hit before we go in?" I asked, referring to some coke I had.

"Of course. I was wondering when you were going to ask." Maria said.

We both indulged while sitting in the car and allowed the euphoria to overtake us.

"Nice," she said after taking a hit.

"I'll go check it out; you wait." I exited the car, walked up to the door, and read the sign over the bell that simply said Ring for Assistance, which I did. Moments later, a voice came over the intercom requesting me to present my full name.

"Jordan Baros," I said. "Is this the Fur Emporium?"

The voice at the other end responded positively and again asked for my name.

"Jordan Baros. I'm with Maria Velez; we have an appointment."

"One minute, sir. I will check," the female voice said. "Yes, Mr. Baros, you'll be seeing James Douhan. I'll buzz you in, and the hostess will assist you."

"Thank you."

I turned and motioned to Maria to come along. I held the door until she reached the building. We entered through a second set of unlocked doors into a beautifully appointed receiving area designed in an art-deco South Beach style that contained a circular desk, a mixture of contemporary and antique furniture, and brightly colored fashion posters with top models wearing designer furs against a backdrop of teal-colored walls.

"Hello, Mr. Baros, my name is Lina," said a woman sitting behind a desk. "I'm your hostess. Mr. Douhan, our salesperson, is wrapping up with a customer and will be right with you."

"Okay, thank you," I said, still a little disoriented by the dramatic change from the building's exterior to this inner sanctum of opulence and nouveau-riche style. I introduced Maria to the hostess, a striking, olive-skinned, Mediterranean-looking woman with a twinkling small diamond nose piercing, who had now gotten out of her seat and came from around the desk to shake our hands.

Maria was looking as startled as me with the pleasantry of it all but remained cool as Lina sought to make us feel comfortable and like VIPs.

"Why don't you two sit back on the couch and let me get you some complimentary cappuccino and pastries. Or would you prefer some champagne?"

I looked at Maria, who did not hesitate in requesting the champagne. I followed suit by accepting the same.

"I'll be right back. Make yourselves comfortable. Have you been here before?" she asked.

"No," Maria said. "This is the first time. A friend of mine, Wayne George, who played with the Giants, recommended we come."

This was the first time I had heard of Wayne; I thought Stacey, her girlfriend, had recommended this place.

"Oh yes, I know Wayne. I've been to some of his parties in Cliffs Park; he has a condo that overlooks the Hudson. I always love going there!" Lina said excitedly.

"You got it; that's Wayne."

"Well, tell him Lina Quallo was asking about him. I'll be right back with your champagne."

Maria took a seat on the orange-and-burnt-red couch that looked like beanbags sewn together. The couch was covered with patterned silk pillows in vibrant colors inspired from India and Southeast Asia. She picked up the most recent copy of *Vogue* that was resting on a low-rising Chinese coffee table that had sundry other fashion magazines on it.

I sat down and turned sideways, facing Maria with a blank stare.

"What's wrong?" she asked.

"Nothing," I said. "I thought Stacey had set this up. Who is Wayne George?"

"She did. I had called both of them, and they both recommended that we come here, and look, Wayne is an old friend. You're not jealous, are you?"

"No, not jealous. Just uninformed."

"Honey, don't be that way. I don't have anything to hide from you. You know you are my sweetie. Come here, *papi*." Maria placed the magazine on the couch, snuggled up to me, clutched my bicep with her hand, and puckered her lips, beckoning mine to hers. I responded and placed a light kiss on her full, soft lips.

Lina returned and presented us with champagne and pastries. After guessing the brand of the champagne was some high-end Moët or Dom Pérignon, Maria asked Lina, "What is the brand of your champagne?"

Hesitating for a moment and conveying an air of pretense and incredulousness, Lina responded, "Cristal, of course." Quickly adding to that statement to avoid insulting us or giving the wrong impression, she said, "The only time I can indulge is at work; I can't afford this stuff on my salary. I make sure I have at least a glass or two on the weekends."

Maria laughed at Lina's keeping-it-real humor and responded by saying, "I'll drink to that. One more, if you don't mind, and you might as well join us; your day is almost over."

Lina laughed out loud, shaking her head. She went to the other room, brought back a half bottle of Cristal, poured all of us a drink, and placed the bottle on the table. Raising her glass, she offered a friendly toast, saying, "To an attractive couple. May you have a fun-filled afternoon and life of hedonism, full of Cristal and love."

I seconded the toast, and we all tapped glasses and took a drink, continuing to laugh and smile as we imbibed. Shortly thereafter, Mr. Douhan came into the room and introduced himself. Lina interrupted him, apologized for not fulfilling her hostess duties, and continued the introductions.

"Mr. Douhan is one of our leading salespersons, as well as an authority on our products and their designers. He will be able to assist you and answer any questions you have. So with that, it's been my pleasure serving you. Remember to tell Wayne we met, and we'll probably see each other again, if not here, then at some social affair; it's a small world. And hopefully, Maria, you'll be wearing one of our fine shearlings."

"Thanks so much, Lina. It's been great, and of course, I'll tell Wayne how you got us drunk before we started shopping. Good work, girl. One more glass for him might mean a sable or chinchilla for me. You deserve a raise," Maria said.

All three of us laughed except Mr. Douhan, who took Maria seriously and said with a straight face, "That can be arranged."

I didn't say anything but thought, "We'll see; I don't think champagne causes insanity."

"Okay. Shall we get started?" asked Mr. Douhan in a heavy East European accent as he began to assert himself and take the lead. "Let's go to the showroom."

Turning his attention to Maria as we walked down the hallway to the showroom, Mr. Douhan asked, "Do you have anything particular in mind, or are you open to experiencing different types of furs?"

"I have preference for long-haired furs such as raccoon, fox, or mink. Not full-length—something I can wear both casual and semiformal."

"That's good to know. I will give you a brief overview of the different types of furs, their grades, color, texture, and so forth. I'll let you try on some different ones, and I'll also give you time to yourself to indulge. Then we will see what happens. It will be magical how you...how should I say it...fall in love and maybe make your boyfriend jealous."

I had a puzzled look on my face and said, "It's fine; I can handle it."

"Good. Everyone is happy. Now let me tell you a little bit about furs, and you let me know when I talk too much. Fur pelts consist of skin leather, guard hairs, and underfur. Guard hairs are the long, glossy hairs that overlay the shorter, denser underfur. The guard hairs help repel moisture and protect the underfur from damage...underfur serves to protect the skin. It's like layers. Furs from more northern regions are generally more expensive and higher in quality than those from southern regions because of the quality of the underhairs. Another point to remember is *primeness*, which refers to the degree of development of the animal's winter pelt. All furbearing animals undergo at least one annual molt. Summer pelts are thin and flat and are of little or no value as furs. In the fall, as the days begin to shorten, the winter fur grows in."

"How does the amateur determine all this?" I inquired.

"Well, that's my job. I can tell the grade and value of the fur from the manufacturer, the size of the pelts, color and texture, fur density, and length."

"I assume price is also a giveaway."

"Well, of course, the more you pay, hopefully, the better the quality. Any more questions?"

"No. Thanks for the education. That was helpful," I said.

"Are you ready to try on some of our fashions, pretty lady?" Mr. Douhan said to Maria.

"Of course. Let's go," she said.

As we walked to the collections, Mr. Douhan continued his pitch. "We'll start with our designer selections for you to get a feel for some of the most expensive, high-quality items we have. Our featured designers are Oliveri, Christia, Feraud, Krio, and Nicole Miller. For example, Umberto Oliveri began his fashion empire producing haute-couture apparel for the Italian market. During the 1960s, he introduced hand-tailored leather garments. Umberto's children took over after his death and introduced incredible shearling collections. They have long since expanded and are an international favorite for high-quality products. Most film and television stars wear this fantastic collection."

Maria tried a number of selections that were pleasing but not satisfying. She modeled them all for me.

"Why don't you try this mink?" Mr. Douhan suggested, having a better feel for her taste after reviewing her selections and reactions to different coats. With Mr. Douhan's assistance, Maria put on the mink coat he had presented her.

I had taken a seat, and Mr. Douhan and Maria were engaged in a dance as she twirled in front of the mirror. Mr. Douhan, not seeking to commit until the customer committed, made encouraging comments like "You look stunning...fabulous...it matches your complexion and brings out the highlights in your hair."

"What do you think, Jordan?" Maria asked after a period of admiring herself in the mirror.

"It's gorgeous, baby."

Before she could say anything else, I said, "Wait a minute... what's the price of this?"

Almost immediately, Maria said, "I want it," as she turned to face Mr. Douhan.

Mr. Douhan looked as if he didn't know how to react at the spontaneity of the exchange and said in response to my question, "This item is a mere six thousand dollars. But for you, my friend, we can let you have it for half the price; you can't beat that." He then graciously said, "I will leave you two alone to talk." And with that, he stepped aside.

Maria sauntered over to where I was standing, wearing the mink coat, designer jeans, and form-fitting Danskin top, looking as if she had a million dollars in her pocket.

"This is crazy," I said.

"Yes, I know I'm crazy, and so are you. Don't you want me to be happy? And just think how proud you'll feel when we go out and everyone stares at your beautiful girlfriend."

"Yes, I hear you, and you do look good."

"Jordan, I don't ask for much. I'll wear it with nothing but my pink panties you like when you come over. Come on, *papi*, this is for us."

"You deserve it, plus it's your birthday. You sure you want it? Do you want to look around more? Are we being practical? You're gonna need a chauffeur just to wear the coat."

"Now you want me to be practical when you say everything is too practical and you love my spontaneity."

"Okay, baby...be cool. It's yours."

"Thank you, my sweetie! You make me so happy," she said as she kissed me hard and lusciously.

Mr. Douhan appeared, and I told him we would take the jacket.

"Excellent choice," he said.

We eventually left the Fur Emporium. For some strange reason, I felt good having just spent three thousand dollars and seeing how happy I made Maria feel. It was a fascinating afternoon, and our love meter was high. The coke, the champagne, and the mink put us in a rainbow haze.

CHAPTER FOURTEEN

After leaving the Fur Emporium, Maria and I decided to get a bite to eat. She had a craving for Cuban and suggested a cozy place called Little Havana not far from where we were. We were escorted to a room in the back of the restaurant, which was fairly full. The brick walls were adorned with pre-Castro Cuban Revolution paintings and posters. One huge painting showed two Afro-Cuban flamenco dancers twirling carefree in the middle of a group of dignified Caucasian women in long dresses, who seemed to be gazing with disdain at the open jauntiness of the dancers.

Maria had enough champagne earlier and settled for sparkling water with lime. I ordered a Dos Equis beer.

"That place blew my mind," Maria said, referring to the Fur Emporium.

"Did you see my reaction when he said six thousand dollars? Can you imagine—that's what a house costs in some parts of the country," I said.

"What country are you talkin' 'bout—Mexico? You don't think I'm worth that much?" Maria said.

"Let's not go there; it has nothing to do with my feelings for you or your worth."

"I know. Jus' teasing. You are good to me," Maria said, pouting her lips. "Mr. Douhan was good...I mean, his talk about the different furs and pelts. He knows his shit."

"I guess. With all that info, I can go out and trap some animals and make you a coat," I said.

"I know what that would look like—a little squirrel, some mouse, and maybe some raccoon from your yard...you got deer over there; why not throw that in?"

We laughed at our own silliness.

"Now I can get that suede outfit we saw at Charmyne's; I want to wear it next weekend. I wish we could be together. I'm supposed to go with Stacey to a party in Harlem."

"I wish, but I can't. You know how things are. Plus, next week's a big one for me. I've got that project at work and presentation."

"Don't you want to see it?"

"I already did."

"Ooh, yeah, that's right, but I'd like you to be there when I buy it."

"You'll be fine. We'll do something later for your b-day. I'm trying to get tickets to Alvin Alley."

"Okay, but it won't be the same without you...but I understand."

"What are you getting?" I asked Maria.

"Rice and beans and the grilled sea bass. What about you?"

"That sounds good. Red or black beans?"

"I want red with yellow rice," Maria said.

"I think I'll have the black beans and white rice."

Our drinks arrived, and Maria engaged the waitress, who was from Guatemala, in some Spanish chitchat, some of which I understood because it was sprinkled with English. After the waitress left, Maria started to tell me everything they said, some of which I had already interpreted.

I said, "So she misses home but needs to be here because there is no work back there, right?"

"That's good. I'm proud of you, *mi* handsome *amigo.*"

"I want to learn more Spanish. I want you to talk to me in Spanish from now on," I said.

"You know you don't want that. Plus, my broken Spanglish will just confuse you. Anyway, we need to talk seriously. What's happening? How are, uh, things at home?"

"Things are cool. We haven't said much since what I told you. Same ol' things—family, the kids. I was with Chad earlier today before I came to your sister's."

"What is Trina saying?"

"We haven't talked much; she's still questioning me about our future. I know she's making contacts and looking to go back to work. She was at a conference today about new media. All her attention seems focused on getting back to work, maybe to avoid dealing with all the negativity and me."

"Well, that's understandable. But I assume she's going on with her life. Has she or you at least talked about why things are as bad as they are?"

"Yeah, we've had those discussions, and she promises to change."

Maria sardonically added, "That's what they all say; you know that."

I decided to change the conversation away from Trina. "How are you feeling about all this? What are your thoughts?"

"You know what I want, but I don't want to pressure you. I know how important those boys are. I know your wife will never let you go and will use the kids and everything else to keep you or make you miserable."

Being as direct as Maria, I asked, "Why haven't you married? What has stopped you in the past? I know you love kids and all, and I'm sure you've met guys who have offered you anything you wanted. Why never?"

"It's not that easy. Yes, I've been engaged, and I lived with Andre for eighteen months. He would have married me in a heartbeat, but I didn't want that."

"Why?"

"Andre had been married, was still involved with his ex, wanted me to be there to wait on him hand and foot, clean his house, and do his laundry...control freak. He wanted a mother more than a wife. Plus he hated children, so we really never connected that way. He was a rebound for me after I broke up with my detective friend."

"Who was that?"

"I mentioned Marcus to you. He was an NYC detective who used to come by my job after meeting me at a club one night while I was out with some lady friends. He was a wild dude. Cops are the same as the criminals they chase. He got off on drug busts and on handcuffing and beating up folks. He used to let me ride in the car when he was undercover. He showed me how you can tell if someone is packing, things to look for on the street...drug dealers, deals about to go down, all this stuff. And you start to get into that world. He had all these women all over the city and kids by different women, but he was willing to give it all up for me."

"What happened?"

"I don't know. After all the talk and promises, he never really did anything to make it happen. For all I know, he was probably still married. I felt as if I was becoming a part of his stable."

"What's this with you and married men?"

"I don't choose them; it just happens."

We continued to talk while we ate. Maria spoke of other failed romances and lost loves and confessed that she had dated Wayne George, who recommended the Fur Emporium.

"Haven't you had the urge to want to commit—even if it isn't perfect—for the sake of having children and starting a family? Some people call it 'settling,'" I said.

"Well, I have committed on a few occasions. And hopefully you won't judge me harshly, but I'm thirty-four, not a virgin, and have been pregnant on three occasions—most recently, before I met you, with Andre's baby. If I hadn't miscarried, I would have probably done exactly what you said. Luckily, once I lost the baby, I knew it was over. I've also had two abortions," Maria said, as a teardrop rolled down her left cheek. She sat back in her chair and grabbed her napkin to hold under her right eye, catching the other drop.

CHAPTER FIFTEEN

I was overwhelmed by the time I dropped Maria off at her sister's house. Given all that transpired that day, it was no wonder. Ordinarily I would have gone to her place in Brooklyn or gotten a room in the city, but after we left the restaurant, desire was on empty. Throughout the time with Maria, I always did a comparison of the two relationships, my marriage and my affair, measuring one against the other based on their respective qualities, as if keeping some kind of scorecard.

After today's talk at Little Havana's, I had a letdown. Questions infected my mind. Maybe I was too naïve and caught up in the erotic fantasy, or Wanda was right, and I was being used like the others who had fallen for Maria's game. Maybe she did put her menstrual blood in my food. On the other hand, her promiscuity was a contrast to my tame relationship with Trina. Maria was a stallion, who excited my ego and made me desire to possess and control her. Then there was the loving and devoted "good girl." Trina was a virgin when we met and had never been with another man. I couldn't recall her even showing interest in another man.

CHAPTER SIXTEEN

I t was very late by the time I got home. As I pulled into the drive-way, the popping and crunching of the gravel stones under the car tires were amplified against the silence of the early morning. It was about 4:00 a.m. and wintry cool as the wind whistled through the partially barren tree branches. Dawn was beginning to offer fractured bits of illumination.

"Hopefully, Trina is sleep and won't hear when I enter," I thought. I walked up to the front door, inserted the key, and slow-ly opened the door. The squeaks and mechanical sounds of the hinges, metal on metal, which go unnoticed during normal times, sounded as loud as a freight train carrying a cargo through a rural farmland. I entered and proceeded straight up the squeaky stair-well to the bedroom. My eyes adjusted to the darkness, and I could see that Trina was not in bed.

Before I finished turning on the reading lamp next to the bed, I heard someone coming up the stairs. The footsteps were unabashed and roaring with pronouncement as they came closer. She must have been sitting in the living room when I entered the foyer, I surmised. Trina entered the bedroom with anger etched across her brow.

"Where have you been? What are you trying to do to me?" she asked.

I began my lie. "At work. You know I have that presentation this week."

"What are you talkin' 'bout? I called your office. Who works until four o'clock on a Sunday morning? Don't take me for a fool, Jordan. I know more than you think. What do you intend to do? What about us…why?"

I thought, "Is she probing? What does she mean, 'I know more than you think'?"

"I can't answer your questions because I don't know what you are talking 'bout. We agreed that we have to be more considerate of each other. We talked last week, and I intend to do better. I'm under a lot of pressure right now. What do you want from me?"

"Please, Jordan, don't…don't do this to us, not after everything we've been through. It's not fair…think about it, what you are saying. I could kill you right now…don't humiliate me, yourself, your children…our family. You have turned everything we stand for into a lie."

Trina's vitriol started to subside, and her tone became reasonable, pathetic, and fatalistic. "I tried to ignore my intuition. I've known for some time things weren't right, but I chose to ignore my gut feelings and focus on things I could control, like getting back to work and household things." A peculiar calmness was evident in her facial expression—a half smile and smirk of disgust.

We both sat on the edge of the bed, and Trina held her head in her hands. I stared intently at the wall. She looked at me and said, "What are we going to do?"

I wasn't convinced that she knew anything specific or if Wanda had spoken to her. She was probably speculating. I was not about to confess. "I don't know. I think counseling might be something we should look into."

"I can't continue like this. Maybe we need some time apart to get our thoughts together."

"No, I don't want to leave you. Jared and Chad—they need me, and I need them. I can't be a weekend parent...we'll talk about it."

With that, I got up from the bed and said, "It's best I sleep in the other room."

Trina was crying and came toward me, wanting to be held. I held her, but we slept in separate beds that early Sunday morning. We agreed it was best for the kids if we maintained normalcy until we decided what we were going to do.

CHAPTER SEVENTEEN

It was a new workweek. The silence at home since our talk was unnatural and eerie; neither of us could muster the strength to say anything more. The hurt was pronounced and internalized; emptiness gnawed at my insides, and I assumed the same was true for Trina. She bit her lower lip and frequently twitched her nose, an idiosyncrasy of hers during times of stress. I was nonexistent to her. All I got from her was revulsion and disgust.

I continued to sleep in the adjacent bedroom. I left the house each morning compartmentalizing my emotions, turning cold and directing my attention on work. The week was consumed with preparations for Thursday's board meeting. I stayed late and called home to let Trina know where I was and what I was doing. I spoke to Maria on breaks and handled the arrangements Stacey had asked for regarding the "delicacies" for the party, but for the most part, I was fully engaged with work and meetings.

Today was the day. I awoke this morning after finally falling to sleep fairly late. The anxiety and stress of the thought of today's presentation made me restless earlier in the evening but finally gave way to tiredness and allowed for a moderately restful sleep. I hate alarms that jolt you out of sleep like an electric shock to start the day, but given the magnitude of the occasion I erred on the side of caution and set the alarm the night before. Last thing I needed was to be late to work. And I was jolted awake at seven this morning to begin the day.

I had selected the suit and tie I would wear the night before. Conservative, corporate, navy-blue suit, white shirt, and red Ivy League striped tie blended with black, wing-tipped Johnston & Murphy shoes. The right image can be almost as important as the substance of the presentation. The attire bespoke *winner* at the start.

I recited my talking points out loud while getting dressed and role-played as if one of the officers on the board were asking a particular question. I continued this exercise silently, I think, on my way to work and during the walk up from Penn Station to the office.

The meeting was scheduled for ten o'clock in the corporate boardroom on the top floor of the fifty-story skyscraper Federal Retail occupied. It was eight thirty when I arrived, which gave me time to do some last-minute organizing and gather materials before I went upstairs. I wanted to speak with my assistant attorney, Ryan Douglas, who had been assigned to the project. There was the issue of the inactive savings and loan that Federal owned, and no one had conclusively determined whether it was an impediment to the broker-dealer activities. Winthrop did not address it in its report, and Ryan had not gotten back to me with any conclusions from his research.

When I entered his office, he said, "How are you feeling, Jordan? This is the big day."

"I'm ready as I'll ever be. I know it's not the right analogy, but I think I know what it's like on death row, waiting for the execution."

"You'll do fine; I have five bound copies of the presentation to carry in with you. The board received their copies yesterday at noon and the executive summary you prepared, so all the details are complete."

"What about the issue that came up in the beginning regarding the savings and loan? I never received anything about that. Is it an issue or not?"

Ryan paused for a moment, looking upward, as if the answer were on the ceiling. "I spoke to Richard Perillo in regulatory, and his opinion is that as an inactive license, it's a nonissue."

"But what about the future? I don't know what the board's future intent is with this bank. Do I box them in with this proposal? They spent big money and time with that acquisition and filings."

"I'll have to check with strategic planning or Sid Amond, who handles these complex financial activities and future plans."

"You mean I have to go before the board in one hour and something that I asked about months ago is still unsettled?"

"I'm sorry—there are so many things going on, I thought Perrillo's lack of concern was the answer."

"That's not good enough. Go talk to Sid and see what you get." I abruptly left and went back to my office. As I entered, the phone rang, and it was Ted Doran, my boss.

"Hi, Jordan. Just wanted to check in and see how things were going. I'll be in the boardroom for the presentation, sitting behind you in the first row. Lawrence will be at the table with you. Are you ready?"

"Yes, sir. We've put a lot of effort into this, and I still think it makes good business sense for Federal. Hopefully, the board will see it as we do."

"Well, good. You'll do fine, I'm sure. Good luck, and I'll see you up there."

I knew it was better not to show any doubt or lack of confidence at this juncture. Anyway, what could Ted do now? The show had to go on, and hopefully, the bank issue would not be the Achilles' heel that undermined the deal.

I arrived in the boardroom at nine forty-five; it was still only partially filled with some corporate executives and interested employees sitting around the perimeter of the room about eight feet from the expansive board table. The agenda listed me going first, which was good. My presentation was scheduled for about thirty minutes, including questions and answers. I would present for about fifteen minutes and then open it up for questions. That was how I hoped it would go, but I knew the board would never let me finish, and I could expect to be peppered with questions within two to three minutes into the presentation. The majority of the board, top officers, and directors had undiagnosed attention deficit disorder, were incessant talkers and know-it-alls, and were rude and arrogant people, so it would be impossible for them to listen, be courteous, and learn before speaking. Different from courtroom presentations, the theme in business is brevity and the bottom line. Judges and juries are a lot more tolerant and are required to absorb more detail than a room of corporate executives, who want just enough information to make an informed decision and know whatever decision they make will not put them in jail.

I was more accomplished as a courtroom speaker, having been a criminal prosecutor before joining Federal, but I knew the distinction. I had prepared my presentation based on the standard mantra—Tell 'em what you are going to tell 'em…tell 'em…and tell 'em what you just told 'em.

I worked the room, acknowledging those I knew and introducing myself to those I didn't. I showed confidence, talking sports, politics, some personal issue, or other small talk when an opening presented itself. I was cool and collected. Introverted by nature, I can do this for a limited time; it just takes more out of me than an extrovert, who might be energized by this type of people interaction. By the time I got back to my chair, the board table was three-quarters filled. President Richard Willis was sitting to the right of Chairman Jeff Tatum at the head of the table, and various senior executives, including the CFO, COO, and senior vice presidents, were situated in order of descending power. When I was called to speak, I would be at the opposite end of the table, facing the chairman. But for now, I was seated on the perimeter, waiting.

Chairman Tatum began the meeting requesting approval of the prior meeting's minutes, engaging in some banter and inside jokes with other members of the board. Before asking me to begin my presentation, he gave a brief introduction regarding Federal's opportunity to diversify its product offerings and gave compliments to the head of the Financial Services Department for its accomplishments. The vice president returned the compliment, saying that the accomplishments were a result of the unyielding support of the board and Chairman Tatum's and President Willis's leadership, blah, blah, blah.

Finally, I was acknowledged. As I stepped forward, Lawrence Whitney of Winthrop & Hudson joined me.

"Mr. Whitney, I haven't seen you in a while—not since the Cindy's Chocolate franchise deal in Belgium last year," the chairman said to Lawrence.

"And be assured, Mr. Chairman, you have been missed also. But after spending six months back and forth, and with all the chocolate I indulged, I thought it best I stay away, at least to try to lose the twenty pounds I put on."

Reacting to the humor of the statement, everyone laughed in unison.

"You deserve the best; you did a fantastic job for us."

"Thank you, Mr. Chairman," Lawrence said.

"Mr. Baros, I understand you have some good things to tell us, I hope. Why don't we get started?"

"Thank you, sir. First let me introduce myself, since this is my first time before the board. I am a senior attorney working with Ted Doran in the Diversified Services Division of the Legal Department. As you are aware, we are counsel to the corporate Financial Services Department and various related divisions, including new business for our insurance subsidiaries."

I quickly moved from the preliminaries to the substance and easily found my gait. Surprisingly, I was five minutes into the delivery before being stopped by Richard Willis, the president, who was slumped in his chair. He began by characterizing my presentation as factual and technical, all of which he understood and appreciated, before he asked his question.

"What is the bottom line? How does operating a money-market fund benefit a retailer whose only other similar activity is insurance—if one can call that a related activity?"

"Understood, President Willis that is a very good question," I said, realizing I would have to fill in other essential information around questions asked because the game and momentum were about to shift, and I would have to manage the shift and maintain some semblance of control. This second half would also determine the final score.

Answering the question and sounding confident, I listed the positives, including formation of a subsidiary to provide fee-based investment advice and distribution of fund shares, acting as a vehicle for the insurance companies and offering customers a competitive yield on insurance settlements from policies, and augmentation of the retail credit-card services and those receivables by offering debit cards tied to customer money-market accounts, which would increase cash purchases at the Federal stores.

The board was abuzz now with side conversations as other transaction-related questions were asked and responded to artfully. I knew I was on point and had hit the mark.

Lawrence stated his confirmation of the potential. "Legally, this deal has legs but must be carefully structured to avoid any undue burden or securities-regulation scrutiny that jeopardizes or unduly burdens corporate management, particularly the retail component. We have outlined those issues in our legal analysis."

Some twenty minutes into the presentation and near its end, Chairman Tatum was still uncharacteristically silent and poker faced, listening to all the questions and responses. Eventually, he spoke.

"Well, I commend you, Mr. Baros, on a fine delivery of information to this board. And you know that I am a retail man; this has been my life since I started with this company as a buyer more years ago than I like to think about. You also know that it is hard to teach an ol' dog new tricks…and when we started down this path some years ago, I was against anything that wasn't retail. For one thing, I don't understand half the things we have moved into, and that being what it is…I admit I was wrong, and the company has done well by itself. Can't say I understand all the things you told me today… but that's all right; that's what I pay all you smart people for."

Leading up to his point, this wily warrior continued. "Now I know about three years ago, this board approved the purchase of a bank, and I continue to wait to see what it is we intend to do with that institution…but a lot of money and time was dedicated to that matter. I also recognize that I'm the oldest person in this room, and I say this with pride, also realizing that half of you were not born during the Great Depression, except for maybe you, Richard. You can't be that far behind me." The chairman looked directly at President Willis, who had a goofy Disney-character look on his face as the other board members chuckled at this moment of levity.

"Be that as it may," the chairman continued, "there did exist, and I assume it still does, a law called the Glass-Steagall Act. Now, this law was enacted to avoid the catastrophe that occurred during the thirties, when banks were securities dealers and customers' money and bank money were invested in the market, and when the market collapsed, it all went down in a heap to hell in a handbasket. Now with all that said...tell me, Mr. Baros, what am I missing?"

The one point I was most vulnerable on was about to hit the fan like shit in a closed closet, and there was no way to avoid it. Ryan, my legal associate, was conspicuously absent and never got back with anything that would allow me to hang my hat on to escape the noose around my neck. Lawrence, sitting next to me during the chairman's formulation of the question, had his head down, writing notes to himself.

"Mr. Chairman, your question raises a very interesting issue," I said.

Before I could finish, Lawrence said, "Glass-Steagall only relates to banks that are members of the Federal Reserve System. Is that the case with the dormant bank you own?"

For a brief moment, I felt a sense of redemption. "I could kiss the yarmulke-looking bald spot on Lawrence's head, this brilliant son of a bitch," I thought. But salvation did not last long because someone at the table confirmed the fact that the bank was a federal savings and loan and a member of the Federal Reserve.

All eyes again refocused on me. Reeling from the jolt of exhilaration followed quickly by depression, I felt wobbly and stretched to give a cogent answer to the question. "I apologize, Mr. Chairman, but this information...ah...you have presented has not been fully investigated, and...ah...I will need some time to confidently answer your question."

"You mean to tell me that you have not factored such a critical piece of information into your analysis? How can that be?"

"With all that is involved and the due diligence that we were required to engage in, it somehow got...ah...lost in the process, even though it was part of discussions early on."

"What about that, counsel?" The chairman directed his inquiry at Lawrence.

"As you know, Mr. Chairman, our firm has represented Federal for decades but was not party to the bank purchase because of a conflict with other clients we represent. Saying that, we were also not presented with any information as to status of the bank or any plans regarding strategic initiatives. Our analysis was confined to the facts as they relate to Federal's retail and insurance operations. I'm more than willing to explore ways to address the act and try to structure the securities and banking activities in a way that avoids Glass-Steagall prohibitions."

"That's not true!" I thought. "I specifically asked Lawrence and John Billing at our meeting to make sure that the money-fund transaction did not conflict with other business ventures Federal might be engaged in, and they assured me they would. What a fucking weasel! Besides, Lawrence knows he's untouchable—he's part of 'the good ol' boys' network.' He's probably related to the chairman; his father's probably the chairman's best friend and country-club golf buddy. Who knows? That SOB just threw me under the bus!"

"Well, this does not make me feel good. It seems there's a lot of work to be done. Mr. Baros, when did you intend to let us know your work was incomplete? Also, when do you intend to finish it? Hopefully, you weren't going to let me spend shareholders' money before you informed us that there might be a problem."

"Not at all, Mr. Chairman, and I...ah...apologize again, but I'm sure this issue can be overcome and will not jeopardize the money-fund initiative or future banking activities."

"Hopefully, that is the case. For now, I think we have exhausted this matter. I look forward to further discussion in the future."

I was exposed and naked, feeling alien to everything that was happening. My paranoia said the whole room was talking about me and the slap down that had just occurred. I wanted out, needed to catch my breath…and hide.

After being dismissed, I approached Lawrence outside the boardroom. He began by saying, "Well, that did not end the way I would have liked, but we'll straighten it out. I'll talk to the chairman during the break to see where he wants to go with this."

Still half-dazed, I responded with, "Okay, Lawrence, we'll talk later. I need to regroup."

"Don't worry about it. I've seen worse; these things go through all kinds of filters and analysis before they go live. It's just the process…it will be fine."

"Encouraging," I thought, "but it does little to lift my spirits. Plus, why should I trust Lawrence? Once he has his one-on-one with the chairman, they'll both seek to destroy me. Lawrence will position himself as the hero to correct my incompetence. I know how these folks operate."

Ted Doran, my boss, was nowhere to be found. "Not a good sign," I thought. Plus, no one else came up to offer support or encouragement. Different from when I worked the room prior to the presentation and touched their flesh—now there was no one to be found. If I could have become invisible and slipped away, that would have been the best solution.

"Good job, Jordan," said Judy, my secretary, as we entered the elevator to go back to our office.

"Thanks, Judy, but I don't think the chairman liked it."

"Oh, don't say that. You did your best."

"That's the weakest compliment someone one can give, particularly to a person whose best is never good enough," I thought.

CHAPTER EIGHTEEN

If the board lynching was not bad enough, I was caught completely unsuspecting when I arrived home that evening. As soon as I entered the house, I was met by June, our housekeeper, who had an anguished look on her face.

In a more pronounced West Indian accent than normal, she informed me, "Trina and da boys gone to stay with Ms. Lewis. I goin' home, and Ms. Trina said...you would take me to da bus, okay?"

I was totally perplexed, and my brow was more wrinkled than a Shar Pei dog. I shook my head in confusion while extending my neck and looking directly down at June—as if this motion would clarify what I was trying to comprehend. I was sure my body language made her even more nervous.

"When did she leave?"

"Dis afternoon, she come from work and gits da boys at school. Is tings okay? This is vexing."

She was an immigrant from Trinidad, undocumented, with good instincts and common sense. We had made a conscious effort to shield the boys from what was happening, and indirectly we had shielded June, we thought. But I know June had detected something, whether she knew the complete details or not. But I was not about to discuss my marriage with the housekeeper.

"Okay, I'll take you to the bus. Are you ready?"

"Yes, I get me tings from da kitchen."

I dropped June off at the bus stop and told her Trina would call next week to let her know when she should come back.

"Awright, Mr. Jordan...uh, tell da boys I'll see dem later, and you be careful," June said, with a tone and look of concern.

"I will, and you be careful getting home. Bye."

My mind was racing, and there was an unrelenting sharp pain in my stomach, causing a gastrointestinal discomfort and reflux that made me burp involuntarily. "Get it together," I said to myself. "Should I head to Hazel's house? I don't want to go there and have to deal with Trina and her mother. Go home. Call her. Talk about what's happening. What about the boys? This is a big mess."

I ran up the stairs when I got back to the house. Sure enough, Trina had taken a bunch of her clothes out of the closet and packed them. I looked on her nightstand to see if she had left a note but didn't see anything. The phone rang, and in my haste, I jerked the cord and pulled it off the nightstand. It hit the carpet and bounced. I bent over to pick it up as I answered the call.

"Hello...hello."

"Yes...Jordan, it's your mother. What was all that noise?"

"I knocked the phone off the table."

"You sound out of breath. Are you all right?" my mother said, probably detecting an unusual inflection in my voice and the heavy breathing.

"Yeah, I'm fine...I guess. How are you?"

"Okay for an ol' lady. I haven't spoken to you lately...you never call."

"Ma, Trina moved out. I came home from work, and she and the boys were gone. June said they went to her mother's house."

My mind was still racing with anxiety, bordering on panic. I had not expected my mother Rachel when I picked up the phone but was glad to speak to her. My panic and state of mind were transferred to her, and she reacted with the same level of anxiety.

"Oh my God! What is happening? Well, it doesn't shock me. Last I spoke to her, she didn't sound good. Have you spoken to her?"

"No. I was about to call her when you called."

"Your sister is finished with you. She told me everything. What has gotten into you? You've changed. You have so many blessings, and you are just throwing them away. It's all about material things, and you've lost sight of the real values—your family. You are turning your back on everything that has made you the person you are. Think about it…do you even know what is happening?"

I felt as if I were on the verge of a huge car wreck on a dreary, foggy night on a congested foreign interstate, heading right into the collision. I could see it coming—the loss of control, the lights flashing, the sounds of horns and tires screeching as drivers sought to avoid the wreckage, and then the magnetic pull into a soundless kaleidoscope of streaking lights and the painless rumble of a cataclysmic impact.

I had to get off the phone with her; she was not helping the situation. I held this subconscious anger against her. I was getting angry, annoyed, and irritated with her and Wanda. Anger was supplanting my anxieties. "How dare she pass judgment on what I have become, as if she isn't responsible for whoever I am?" I thought. The nature and timing of my mother's statements set me off. I had always had deep-seated childhood emotions from my father's abandonment…my relationship with her…feelings of being unloved, compounded by her marriages and abuse by my stepfather. I always questioned our bond—its security and our love—and I always came up wanting. "Fuck Wanda," I thought. "I know she is the cause of this. I'm sure she told Trina about Maria."

"How dare you pass judgment on me and who it is you think I am? You don't know me and never have," I blurted out in a direct assault on my mother's sensibilities. Catching myself before I lost all control, I said, "Look, this not the time for us to discuss our relationship. We do need to have that talk, but for now, I need to speak with Trina and find out what's happening. I will call you later."

"Don't you talk to me that way. I'm your mother. I'm only trying to help. I did the best I could for you. Just promise me you don't hold this against your sister. She did what she thought was right. We are family," Mom said, with a pleading tone in her voice.

"I'm not worried about Wanda, and she needs to mind her business. I will deal with her later. I have to go. I need to talk to Trina."

"You go and call Trina, and I'll talk to you later."

I hung up and didn't deliberate on the conversation with my mother. I began to rummage through Trina's nightstand to find Hazel's phone number; I didn't call my in-laws often. Eventually finding the number, I dialed it. I uncharacteristically failed to consider beforehand what I was going to say. I was speechless and caught by surprise when Hazel answered the phone.

"Hello," she said.

I stumbled momentarily, and absent of any small talk given the situation, I struggled with what to say to get past Hazel so I could speak with Trina. Not coming up with anything, I said, "Hi, Hazel, uh…is Trina there?"

Doing better than me, Hazel said, "What is wrong with you? Your children need you, and all this foolishness makes no sense."

"I know. That's why I'm calling. I want to speak with Trina. How are the boys?" I was cowering somewhat from Hazel's bluntness.

"The boys are fine; they're eating dinner. Trina is upstairs in her room." Abruptly, Hazel stopped the conversation. I could hear over the muffled sound caused by her hand covering the speaker that she called Trina to pick up the phone.

Finally answering after what seemed like an unusually long time, Trina said, "Yes," with a subdued tone.

"Hi, how are you?" I said.

"Okay. Tired."

"I came home, and June told me you had gone to your mother's. I took her to the bus stop and called. When did you decide to do this?"

Reacting impatiently, Trina said, "What do you expect me to do? Just be your doormat?"

"No, I didn't mean it like that. We were talking about things... I...uh...thought we had decided to try to work on things...I just didn't expect to come home and find you and the kids gone."

Trina half choked on every word said to me. "I love you, always have, but I'm concerned about us...I don't trust you, and I don't want to play games with my life. If you don't want to share your life with me anymore, so be it. It's better to make up our minds now than to live a lie that will only bring pain and misery. I'm not as strong as you. I can't get up each day and go to work and carry on as if nothing is happening. Your strength has always been something I admired, but when it's turned on me, I can't take it."

"I can't take it, either. I'm not this empty shell you say I am."

"You need to get your act...life together; maybe me and the kids not being there will be good for you. I don't know what to do...are you trying to kill me?"

"No, I'm not trying to kill you. I love you and the boys."

Somewhat incredulously, Trina said, "That's the first time I've heard you say that to me in a long time. Why do you do this? Am I supposed to believe you now? Act like nothing has happened?"

"No, I wouldn't expect you to do that. I just don't want to lose everything."

"You need to make up your mind. I know everything, and don't blame your sister for your acts—she is doing what she thinks is best. You can't have everything, and if you are willing to risk it all for that bitch, you had better be ready for the consequences. I can't continue this conversation; it upsets me too much…I'll talk to you later." Trina hung up the phone.

I sat on the edge of the bed and put the phone down, finally hanging it up after the screeching disconnect alert disoriented me. I hadn't eaten all day but wasn't hungry. I lay on the bed in a fetal-like position under the comforter, with my knees touching my chest. With no appetite and a cascade of voices in my head, I had an urge to scream. I visualized myself running down the street naked, screaming unintelligible clatter at the top of my lungs. "Am I insane?" I wondered. Trina had expressed, on occasion, concern about my mental state. I even ridiculously debated the issue.

What defines insanity? Just because it's not conventional, does that make one insane? Why can't someone love two women? What if each offered something different? There are societies that recognize arrangements that are not monogamous. So my insanity is limited to certain places?

CHAPTER NINETEEN

Maria was finishing up her primping for the evening, donning her eyeliner by pulling tightly her left eyelid with her left index finger, thereby getting maximum exposure before applying eyeliner with the right hand. She reached into her purse and removed a tube of Estée Lauder rose lipstick, formed a rounded mouth, and applied it to accentuate her full lips. She moved into her bedroom to see herself in the larger mirror and was pleased with the image. She was striking this evening and knew it. The black suede pantsuit with a waistline jacket she recently bought fit marvelously and emphasized her rounded hips, fitting as snugly as the satin pushup bra and thong underwear she wore underneath her outfit. Her hair was long, just below her shoulders, and diamond studs sparkled in her earlobes as she tossed her hair. The energetic crescendo of Chaka Khan's music was pumping from her stereo, as was the excitement flowing through her veins. She added the final touches and lightly splashed her upper chest, wrist, and neck with Pheromone perfume. After she finished, she took another glance at her posterior in the mirror now that she had put on the same Christian Louboutins she had worn to bed last time she and Jordan made love. The thought sent a pleasant rush through her as she gave a high-pitched "Ooouchh!" after slapping her own rear with the palm of her hand. About this time the phone rang; it was Stacey.

"Hey, girl, you ready? I'm on my way and should be there in fifteen."

"Good. I'm ready, I'll meet you downstairs. Ring the bell. Don't try to park; I'll look out for you."

"Okay. Whatcha wearing?"

"You'll see; it's an outfit I bought at Charmyne's—you know, that li'l boutique we like. It's fabulous, girl. You'll see."

"I know it must be fine. Are you wearing the fur?"

"You'll see. I'll show you when you get here."

"I'll be right there. See ya in a minute."

About fifteen minutes later, the bell rang, and Maria grabbed her new mink jacket and black leather purse, which accentuated the total look, and headed downstairs to meet Stacey.

Once in the car, the girls exchanged compliments on their outfits. Stacey, who was pleasingly ample up top, was wearing a pair of black gabardine pants with a gold-sequin top that left nothing to the imagination because of the plunging neckline. They were both hot and knew it. The excitement filled the car, and the chitchat was nonstop. Maria went on to explain what had happened at the Fur Emporium as Stacey continued to admire her mink.

"I need to start looking out for myself, find me a man like Jordan, and stop giving it away for free," Stacey said.

Maria didn't say anything but was thinking that Stacey's problem with relationships was her obvious neediness. She left nothing to the imagination and put it all on the table as soon as she met a guy she liked. Maria preferred a more subtle, long-term strategy with a touch of independence.

"You know, I thought about giving you a surprise party; I'm so sorry I didn't," Stacey said, giving cover to what was planned that evening.

"Don't worry about it. No big deal. Plus, I prefer it this way...I'm going to party tonight and just have a good time."

"Too bad Jordan's not coming. Have you spoken to him?"

"Yeah, briefly Friday. He was sounding kinda funny; he didn't say why, but I think it was his job. He had a big presentation, and I don't think it went well. I didn't see him all week."

"I'm not going to go there, but I hope you don't get all uptight tonight. There are gonna be some fine dudes at this party, trust me."

"Bring 'em on, girl. Mami got somethin' for them."

They both shrieked, Maria turned the car radio up louder, and they sang karaoke to "Reasons" by Earth, Wind & Fire.

Stacey pulled up to an elegant-looking brownstone on West 123rd Street and Malcolm X Blvd. Gentrification was beginning to take hold in Harlem. It was a risky venture, and crack was becoming an epidemic in the neighborhoods. For the faint of heart, it was probably not the time to move there, but for other risk takers, you could get a lot more for your money above 110th Street than below. Sharon and Jerome Williams, the owners, were a young, ambitious black couple. Sharon was a gynecologist with a small private practice and privileges at Harlem Hospital. Her husband, Jerome, was a marketing rep with a major recording label. Their place was impressive, given their relatively young ages. It was a seven-room, three-bathroom duplex with high ceilings and elegantly draped window treatments.

Maria and Stacey were fashionably late so as to make a grand entrance. You could feel the mood switch as they both entered the large living room, where couples and singles stood in small groups, sipping on drinks and engaged in conversation.

"Let me take your coats," Sharon said. "What a beautiful mink jacket! It feels so soft. And nice outfit," she said after receiving Maria's coat. "Is that suede? I saw a similar outfit in Saks; it must have cost you a fortune. It's just delightful. I feel underdressed."

"Thanks, Sharon. You are so sweet. It's a gift," Maria said.

"Lucky you," Sharon said.

About this time, Stacey removed her coat, and Sharon jokingly remarked on her plunging neckline. "You sure you want to take that off, girl? It could get chilly in here, or maybe you'll raise the temperature with that hot number. Go on, girl. You are smokin' hot!"

Both Maria and Stacey knew they had captured their audience. Even the otherwise calm brothers had momentarily stopped what they were doing to discreetly watch the girls disrobe. The not-so-cool brothers stared with no shame or apology, and the women enviously stole glances or fleetingly cut their eyes to measure the competition as the girls entered the game. The pretty divas deceptively glanced at the duo, trying to assess the threat to the mantle of "boss bitch" by the new entrants. With confirmation of their exalted status, evident by the unspoken and spoken reaction of the crowd, Maria heard one of the men say to another, "Check out this shit, man," as they eased their way into the mix.

"This is a lovely place you have, Sharon," Maria said.

"Oh, you haven't been here before. I know you have, Stacey. Let me show you around. It's a work in progress. Follow me as I hang up the coats."

Sharon placed the coats in a nearby closet and continued into a parlor room past groups of people standing with drinks and having intense conversations with occasional bursts of laughter over a witty comment or comedic incident of mutual appreciation. The party was moderately crowded, so it was easy to maneuver. There was no telling what it would be like as the evening progressed.

In the parlor a bartender was mixing drinks. To the side a buffet of food in silver chaffing dishes artistically placed on a long banquet table with a checkered red tablecloth. The buffet featured the best of New Orleans cuisine—red beans, rice, fried chicken, shrimp and crawfish pasta, chicken and sausage jambalaya, Creole gumbo, cornbread, a raisin bread pudding, and other assorted desserts.

"Are you hungry?" Sharon asked, not looking at either of the girls in particular.

"I think I'll grab a drink and get some food later; the spread looks delicious," Maria said.

"It's all New Orleans cuisine; that's where my dad's people are from. I'm Creole. Friends of ours just opened a restaurant on Lenox and 125th, and they cater. The food is great; we know the owner. He's also from Louisiana…Creole. Have either of you been to New Orleans?"

Maria had not, but Stacey volunteered her Mardi Gras experience, exclaiming that she got drunk and received so many beads that she was walking hunchbacked, wearing them around her neck as she made her way back to the hotel where she was staying.

"The parties and food were out of sight; it was a week of decadence. I have not been back since, and that was about five years ago. I don't think they'll let me back in the state; there's probably a warrant out for my arrest," she screamed with laughter, and Sharon and Maria joined in.

"You are so crazy; you haven't changed a bit. How long have we known each other?" Sharon asked Stacey.

"I met you about ten or eleven years ago. You were in college working as a summer intern at *Essence* magazine, and I was in the Sales and Marketing Department. I knew then you were going places. You were so serious…serious hair, serious clothes… serious man…too damn serious. No one understood why you were at *Essence* and majoring in biology, and you told everyone you were getting in touch with your creative side. That's why we hit it off; you were just what I needed to tone my outrageousness down." Without taking a breath, Stacey segued into a sincere compliment to Sharon. "I'm so proud of you and Jerome. You two are doin' it. Go on, girl, with your bad self!"

Sharon turned and opened her arms to embrace both Stacey and Maria. She whispered in their ears, "I love you, and happy birthday, Maria."

"Thank you, Sharon. I love you, too," Maria responded.

With glasses of white wine in their hands, they proceeded to an adjacent room, where a DJ was setting up and playing some R&B and pop, priming the party for what was to come later—with dance music by such artists as Prince, the Pointer Sisters, Lionel Richie, and Chaka Khan. The eighties music reflected a buoyancy and lightheartedness that contrasted with the socially relevant, consciousness-raising lyrics of the seventies, distinguished by such songs as Marvin Gaye's "What's Going On" and Stevie Wonder's "Innervisions."

"Is that the song by Whitney Houston?" Maria asked as they stood in the dining room, which had been converted to a mini-dance floor.

"Whitney who?" Sharon asked.

A tall, handsome, polished young man looked directly into Maria's eyes, startling her with his sparkling, hazel-eyed penetration. He said, "Right on point. That's Whitney Houston, a new singer with some extraordinary pipes."

"Oh," Maria remarked, still reacting to the intrusion and sizing up the intruder.

About this time, Stacey, who had lagged behind talking with someone she knew, entered the room, and looking in Maria's direction, ran over and almost knocked her down trying to get close to the handsome stranger.

"Reynaldo!" she screamed. "What are you doing here?" They exchanged kisses and hugs.

"Maria, this is my man, Reynaldo Evers—or should I say *Doctor* Reynaldo Evers? We went to college together. Isn't he cute? All the girls at school wanted him. There were about five brothers, all Kappas, the girls wanted." Then to Reynaldo, she said, "You still see that hussy Natalie? You didn't get married on me, did you?"

"Whoa, Stacey, slow down. It's been ages…what's been happening? I haven't seen Natalie since we graduated. I have been so involved with dental school and setting up the practice…I don't get out that much."

"Shuddup, Reynaldo. I know you're lying…I know you too well! You lookin' good…it's so nice to see you."

During this time, Maria was patiently sipping her drink, waiting for the conversation to shift to where it was before Stacey interrupted. Stacey was standing at Reynaldo's right side, with Maria on his left, and said, "Reynaldo, this is my best girlfriend, Maria… have you two met?"

Reynaldo, looking straight at Maria again with those catlike eyes, sharp, angular Latin jaw, and cleft chin, said, "Somewhat. I was just answering a question of hers about the record that's playing. It's this new artist, Whitney Houston. The song is "You Give Good Love." I just picked up the tape. It's sweet, a lot of nice tracks."

Smooth was the word that came to Maria's mind as Reynaldo finished his music review. Maria extended her hand to close the introduction, and he received it not as a handshake but with his palm up and hers lying on top. He gently placed his other hand on top of hers, securing her hand between both of his hands for enough time to communicate sensitivity, strength, and pleasure at meeting her.

"Such soft, strong hands with long fingers, like his six-foot-two frame," she thought.

"Thanks for the recommendation; I'll have to look into it. I've heard it on the radio and keep saying I want to get the album. She's got another song out, doesn't she?"

"Yeah, there's a couple, but trust me—the entire album's good," Reynaldo said, having removed his clasp of her hand.

Sharon was nowhere in sight at this point; she had been called to assist some other guest or was in the kitchen with the help, resolving some party emergency such as no hot sauce or diminishing supplies of cornbread.

"Well, we're checking out the place and all...it's gorgeous. I would love to own one of these brownstones," Maria remarked.

"Where are you now?" Stacey asked Reynaldo.

"I'm in Brooklyn around Prospect Park in the historic district. I own a house there, surrounded by churches I don't attend. It's a quaint neighborhood, the same as it was a hundred years ago."

"I know where that is. I live in Park Slope, closer to Flatbush and Atlantic," Maria said.

"Homegirl...we're neighbors. I've been looking to meet people in the area. We'll have to exchange numbers."

"Sounds good, but you have to excuse me. We have to find Sharon and finish our tour. I'll catch up with you later," Maria said.

"Yes, indeed, Mr. Reynaldo, we will see you later, and make sure you save a dance for me," Stacey added and kissed him on his cheek.

Heading upstairs to see what was happening, Stacey remarked to Maria, "He liked you, girlfriend; he asked for your number."

Acting nonchalant, Maria said, "He just did that because I'm in the area...that was nothing special. How well do you know him?"

Looking at the gleam in Maria's eyes when she asked the question, Stacey didn't hesitate to share his bio. "Dr. Evers got you curious! Look at you, all glowing and stuff, blushing. I haven't seen you like this in a while."

"He is cute...I can't deny that," Maria said, smiling.

"He's cool, likes to party. Mother's from Brazil, father's black, had a beautiful girlfriend in school. She never graduated because of him. He broke up with her, and I think she ended up in some institution."

"What!" Maria exclaimed.

"I don't know if it was an institution—you know how those rumors get started. She was from South Carolina, a stalker type… used to hang outside his dorm in the bushes and shit…waiting for him to come back to the dorm. Finally she just left school…I don't know what happened. Back then I would have jumped on it, except it never happened, and I got to know him too well and all his girlfriends…so we ended up good friends and never crossed to the other side. But I'm warning you—if you don't make that move, I don't know if I'll be able to control these hips and tits. It's been a while, and Mommy is horny as hell."

"Shutyamouth, girl, what are you talkin' about?"

"This is the first time I've seen you react like this in a while, and it's a good sign. Don't get me wrong—Jordan is cool and all, but the man is married, and you ain't getting any younger. I have been through too much with you and your mens. I just don't want you to come out a loser again."

"Leave Jordan out of this…I hear you, but my life is my life, and I'm happy right now, so I'll deal with the future when it gets here. Plus, I do what I do because I want to…I will decide who is in my life or not. I know what I'm doing."

"Okay, *chica* girl, don't go shady on me with that Latina temper. I'm not your enemy. Just don't be closed when an opportunity is right in front of your nose."

"Talking about Jordan, is your friend Nia going to be here, and what is this about Wanda, Jordan's sister you were telling me?"

"You know, I told you I ran into Jordan at South Street Seaport when I was lunching with my friend Nia, and he sat at our table. Nia left; she had to get back to work or something. Later she asked about him, and once I told her his last name, it came out that she went to school with his sister. Your name came up, and I don't know after that."

"Did you tell her about me and Jordan?"

"I don't know what I said. We have talked about you before. You know her; we've all been out together," Stacey said.

"You don't know? Either you told her or not!" Maria said in a high-pitched tone.

"You know how these things are. She put two and two together, I guess."

"You know she told his sister!" Maria exclaimed.

"I dunno that; I'm not involved with all this other shit. This is your life. I doubt that she spoke to his sister."

"Please, are you crazy? I didn't like that bitch when I met her. And yes, it is my life. The rest of you need to stay out and let me live it."

Stacey looked guilty but said nothing.

"Go 'head upstairs…let's see what's happening up there," Maria said, ending the discussion.

Upstairs offered a different atmosphere. There was a master-bedroom suite and two other bedrooms and full bath and a smaller room that probably was a bedroom converted to an entertainment room. From the room, soft jazz was playing into the hallway and brushing against passersby.

"Hi, Jerome," Maria and Stacey both said as Jerome, Sharon's husband, entered the hallway, exiting one of the bedrooms and closing the door behind him. Both Maria and Stacey caught a distinct whiff of marijuana that escaped when Jerome opened the door.

"What's happenin', my sistas?" Jerome responded with a broad grin and dilated pupils.

Both girls followed protocol and kissed him and gave him one-armed hugs so as not to drop their drinks.

"Have you seen Sharon?" he asked.

"Yes, we were with her but lost her; she should be downstairs," Stacey said.

"Who's inside the room?" Maria asked.

"You know—the same folks; they're in there trying some Mexican Gold that Ollie and Rita brought back when they were in Ixtapa and Zihuatenejo last week. It's some good stuff; I got a nice buzz. Go in, but close the door. I'll see you two later. Sharon's probably looking for me. Enjoy."

Maria and Stacey knew some of the folks in the bedroom—college, work, mutual acquaintances, and invariably some new faces. Greetings and salutations were exchanged, some with hugs and kisses, and a special greeting was extended to Ollie and Rita, who had the goodies. Maria and Stacey both sat on the edge of the bed waiting their turn to take a toke on the Mexican Gold Jerome had described.

By the time they were ready to leave, Maria was feeling no pain. Everyone in the room was so nice and funny, as if she had known them her whole life. She couldn't stop laughing. She met an interesting young filmmaker, who kept her in stitches talking about his new movie. He claimed to have worked on set with Woody Allen. The more she smoked, the more he reminded her of Woody, with his large, black, horn-rimmed glasses and funny applejack cap cocked to the side like a character from the TV show *What's Happening*. By the time she left, he had changed from a cute little guy to a black Woody Allen to a bug-eyed human insect of a man—it was hilarious.

The music was pumping downstairs, and the bass was vibrating throughout the brownstone. "It's so loud!" Maria thought. The rhythms were vibrating through her bones as she and Stacey bounced to the rhythm as they walked down the stairs. Prince's new song "Let's Go Crazy" was playing, and the whole place was acting out the lyrics. She didn't think they were gone that long, but the party was packed. The dance floor was full, and they stood on the outside perimeter looking in, waiting for their chance to get their dance on. Maria didn't have to wait long because a familiar hand reached through the crowd and pulled her onto the floor. Someone was blowing a whistle on beat to the music, another group of women were ululating—that long, high-pitched howl expressed by women in Arab, Jewish and African cultures at festive and mournful events. The crowd was insane, and Maria's head was spinning as she joined in.

Leaning closer to her ear to overcome Prince and the party chants and ululations, Reynaldo said, "Party over here...party over there...*chicaa...chicaa*...yeah! I was looking for you."

"We were upstairs; we weren't gone that long, were we?"

"Seemed long to me, probably an hour or more."

Beguiling and coy, Maria responded to his expression of concern with, "You should have come to get me."

Pulling back with a sly smile and getting into his dance, he yelled back, "Next time I'll do that!"

They both smiled, and Maria responded to his moves with some of her own. They were having fun and danced to Tina's "What's Love Got to Do with It," the Pointer Sisters' "Jump" and Lionel Richie's "All Night Long."

Taking a break to clear her head, Maria retired with Reynaldo to the parlor room to get a bite to eat. She was famished from the weed and the dancing—the whole evening was intoxicating. Reynaldo and Maria stood together with plates in their hands, close to the banquet table, where Maria placed her pocketbook.

"I love suede, but it's so hard to keep. Your outfit is sharp," Reynaldo said.

"Thanks. I know what you mean; hopefully, no one spills a drink on me."

"That would be a crime...so tell me what you do," he said.

"I'm in advertising; I work for Galaxy Advertising."

"I've heard of them. What do you do there?"

"I'm in creative and manage a few accounts."

"Any I know of?"

"Probably not. The industry makes you pay your dues. You start at the bottom and remain there and remain there until one day, hopefully, you get a break, or they feel sorry for you. You can change companies...sometimes that opens up opportunities, but hopefully, good things will happen this year. We'll see."

"Yeah, hopefully, this is going to be a better year for me, too. I mean, last year was good, but when you have your own practice, you are only as good as your previous year, so you're constantly trying to do better."

"I'm sure you do quite well. I wish I had one of your years; I'd probably retire."

"I do okay," he said modestly.

Putting his plate down, Reynaldo asked Maria what was upstairs. Without getting into the details, she said people were upstairs "doing their thing and stuff."

"You want to go back up?" he asked.

Maria hesitated at first and didn't respond. Reynaldo followed up by saying, "I don't want to lose you again. Plus, it's quieter up there. We can talk...about Park Slope and all...get to know each other better." He softly added, "Come on, girl."

Maria could not refuse the gesture and placed her plate on the table while picking up her pocketbook. She turned the corner toward the stairs, with Reynaldo following. Once upstairs and after Maria presented the options, Reynaldo suggested that they go into the soft-jazz room; it was unoccupied.

"This is nice and cozy," she remarked. The room was quaint compared to the other bedrooms, nicely furnished with a love seat against the wall, small glass table, a bookcase that contained the stereo equipment, and a writing desk with a leather office chair.

Reynaldo sat down on the love seat and gestured to Maria to join him. "I'm so glad I got to meet you tonight. I've enjoyed it," he said.

"That's good. I enjoyed dancing with you. I can't believe you're right in the same neighborhood as me."

"See, that's fate."

"And on my birthday," Maria said as she sat down.

"I didn't know that, so happy birthday. If I had known, I would have bought you a present."

"Shut up...you didn't even know I was going to be here."

"Let me see...Aquarius, huh?" Reynaldo said.

"On the cusp—Aquarius/Pisces."

"Passionate and assertive...touch of kindness, sometimes moody."

"You forgot beautiful, if you believe all that," Maria said.

"How can I forget the most obvious? I do have something for us to celebrate your birthday. You don't mind if I close the door?" Reynaldo asked politely.

"Go ahead. I can scream, and I know a little karate, if you try to get fresh."

"You won't need either for what I have," he said as he shut the door. He reached into his jacket pocket to pull out a hundred-dollar bill with cocaine wrapped in it.

"Are you down? It's a little something I have." He placed four lines on the glass table.

"No doubt this will be a nice substitute for the present you didn't get me," Maria said jokingly.

"Ladies first," Reynaldo said as he handed Maria a small gold straw-like tool to facilitate their indulgence.

"Oh my God! What a nice touch, sweetie," Maria said in a flirtatious tone.

Maria was no stranger to cocaine. Jordan always had a personal stash. And now, feeling at liberty, she told Reynaldo of her and Stacey's smoking weed earlier when they disappeared and the funny filmmaker she met. It was good for a few laughs.

They both enjoyed a generous line in each nostril. It was good stuff. It flowed from Maria's nose to her toes, which twitched with the euphoric infusion. She instantly experienced clarity of mind coupled with heightened confidence and sensitivity. Very different from the denser, dulling sensation from the weed she had earlier.

"Whew!" Maria said. "That is some good stuff. Doctor, I need a prescription!"

"You liked that, huh? Happy birthday," Reynaldo said. He leaned in to kiss Maria. She was ready but turned her head and offered the cheek. Not too fast—she wanted to keep him guessing and wanting. He accepted the challenge and placed a soft, moist kiss on her cheek, remarking, "I hope at some point there's more."

"Good things come in time," Maria said while placing her hand on his upper thigh. Now she faced him head on and softly kissed his lips, partially opening her mouth but not sharing her tongue or accepting his.

He placed his hand on the indentation of her waist and hips beneath the opened jacket, feeling the smoothness of the suede and the soft, supple frame of her hips.

Captivated by the moment but recognizing the limits, Maria broke the spell and tenderly said, "Sweetie, we had better go downstairs. I need to catch up with Stacey; she's my ride, and I don't know what she's up to."

Reluctant and acting like someone just awakening from a dream, Reynaldo said, "Stacey's fine…I'm sure. Plus, I'll take you home."

"Okay, we'll see. But come on; let's find her first," she said as she got up from the love seat. She extended her hand to Reynaldo, who got up and pulled her to him as he arose, planting another softie on her mouth.

"Come on, now, before you start something you can't finish," Maria said.

"Honey, don't worry about me. I'm fine...I can handle it."

"You're silly. Let's go."

About this time, there was a knock on the door, and lo and behold, it was who else but Stacey.

"Where have you been? I've been lookin' all over for you!" she exclaimed. It was obvious Stacey was in rare form; she was hanging on to the arm of a tall, muscular brother.

"This is Cream," Stacey announced suddenly.

"Kareem, like the basketball player," the muscular man corrected, squinting his eyes at Stacey.

"Cream...Kareem...you my sugar; don't worry about it, sweetie."

At this point Stacey grabbed Reynaldo by the arm, leaving Kareem with Maria, and said, "I need to talk to you, Doc...and what about my dance?"

"We can do that now; we were just coming to get you."

"Weee! Now you two are a couple. I leave you alone for five minutes, and this is how it is."

Kareem and Maria followed Stacey and Reynaldo down the stairs, looking at each other perplexed and wondering, what just happened?

To Maria's surprise, when they got downstairs, everyone was assembled in the dining room. As she entered, Stacey motioned to the DJ, and Stevie Wonder's song "Happy Birthday" started playing. Even though most of the people there didn't know Maria, they sang "Happy Birthday" with the record.

Stacey made a little toast to thank Sharon and Jerome for opening their home and being such wonderful hosts. She expressed her love for and enduring friendship with Maria and jokingly remarked that she was bound through threat of death not to reveal her age. Finally, she presented a beautiful birthday cake to Maria, who took the honor of cutting the first piece. After cutting the first piece, she playfully scooped a fingertip of cream icing and placed it on Stacey's nose.

"I will get you back for this," Stacey said as Sharon handed her a napkin to wipe the cake baptism from her nose.

It was a wonderful evening, and Reynaldo, as promised, drove Maria home when it was over. As they pulled up to her place, she told Reynaldo to park the car, which he did, afterward going around and opening her door. They held hands, and he supported her as they climbed the front steps to go inside.

CHAPTER TWENTY

I t was Sunday, and I had made plans to visit my mother Rachel that afternoon to finish the conversation we started after Trina had left and to cover some other things that were on my mind. The past few years had exposed a lot of raw nerves that demanded attention. I had reached out to Maria early that morning to see how the party had gone but was unable to reach her. I realized that I could have gone to the party, given everything that had transpired since Thursday. I just wasn't in the mood and decided it was best to stay home alone.

⊷⊶

"We need to talk," Mom said as she lit a Salem cigarette. We sat at her kitchen table, and I tried to ignore the obnoxious odor coming from the smoldering matchstick in the ashtray and the plume of tobacco smoke. I love my mother very much, and I'm sure she knows it. However, our family—my mother in particular—are not demonstratively affectionate people. We do not kiss or hug on sight. Affection between my mother and her second husband, Tom, my stepfather, was infrequent to nonexistent, as far as I could remember.

I do recall one occasion that shocked my sensibilities. I was about seventeen years old. We were living in an apartment because Rachel had left Tom and moved out. They had been separated about four months, the marriage having failed to overcome its most recent irreconcilable differences. This was not the first time Mom had moved out. I came home one evening earlier than expected and walked into my mother's bedroom to find her and Tom in the midst of some makeup love that must have exhausted both of them. They were covered with sweat from the passion and were wide eyed and startled when I entered. Embarrassed and shocked, I backtracked in rewind speed out of the bedroom. I climbed the steps to my bedroom in the duplex apartment, ignoring their calls to me, closed the door, and lay on the bed. Two things crossed my mind at that time: I realized that they were going to be a family again and that my parents really did *do it*. It was an amusing moment.

My mother continued her thought as she inhaled another burst of smoke into her lungs and turned her head to the side and upward to exhale into the air the portion that didn't remain in her lungs.

"You know, son, I can't condemn you for what has happened; it's happened before and will happen again. It's as old as the Bible. But I'm concerned about the kids and Trina. I want you to do the right thing by them. Don't make the same mistake I did, thinking your friend is going to make your life better than it is, because she can't."

Reflecting for a moment and looking straight into my eyes, she placed her unoccupied hand over mine on the table. "My dear, I have had three husbands and foolishly left your father and married Tom, your stepfather. I thought he would give me the love and satisfaction your father couldn't. And you know what happened with that; you grew up in that house. I'm telling you this to say I would have been better off if I'd stayed and fought for your father. I'm alone now but for you and your sister, and bless those beautiful grandkids. But the happiness I idealized back then—I don't think about that anymore. Thank God for Earl, my last husband; he died and left a pension and enough money so y'all don't have to worry about me. But it just doesn't happen like that. It doesn't exist, or at least I've never found it. Be sure what you want. You have a good wife and mother to your kids. She loves you dearly, and those qualities are not to be taken lightly and just thrown away. You will appreciate it later when you are my age."

"Ma, I love you and appreciate your telling me this. I know you have my interest at heart. But there are some things I want to say— some not pleasant but necessary—that I think we have avoided for too long."

She nodded her head in reaction to my seriousness and sat back in her chair, giving me the space to present my concerns.

"Sometimes I think I grew up in a world that you want to believe never existed. But you were there. It's part of who we are... our relationship...and it happens to be our truth. I have always felt different—to be blunt, like the stepchild I was. I know now what it means to be a parent, and it is one of the most important callings in life. I have two well-adjusted little boys we all love. They don't question their security or my dedication to them. My extreme dedication is due in part to the lack of commitment I felt when I was young. I have a very good memory; it's an asset and has served me well in school and work. However, it can also be a liability because I don't just remember things that happen; I vividly feel the emotions of a particular event or episode, happy or sad.

"When I think of my childhood, it's with sadness. I was abused. I was the 'dumb nigga' or 'clown,' the 'lazy, good fo' nothin' kid.' Wanda was Tom's daughter, and he was proud of her, the good grades, and the school for gifted children she attended. He would always brag to his friends how smart and beautiful his daughter was. Parents should be proud and supportive of their babies—they need that encouragement to succeed in life. My children have it because I know what it was not to have it. I try to make sure my kids do not experience the loneliness, isolation, and rejection I experienced as a child." I paused at that moment to let Rachel digest what I had just said and also to assess her reaction.

She sat upright and shook her head from what I had just said. "My son, you have no idea what it is like to be a teenage mother with nowhere to turn. I didn't have anyone to show me how to be a mother. I knew I loved you and wanted the best for you. Everywhere I turned, I was rejected. I was alone, and the things I wanted for us couldn't be because I depended on others. Your father cheated on me while at college. I married Tom because I got pregnant with your sister. He gave me forty dollars a week for food, clothing, and everything during our marriage. And yes, Tom had his faults, but they were universal. Everyone was stupid in his eyes…his friends, workers, the grocery clerks…anyone and everyone. Talk about hurt. The things that were said to me hurt to this day. He would tell me he wasn't going to give me anything, but he would take care of the children, and if I didn't like it…there was the door. He said I was like a garbage can, to take his sperm. I was called a secondhand woman. After your father and then Tom, I had no self-esteem left, but I went on trying to do my best for y'all."

"I know, Ma. Things were tough, and you did your best. To hear this makes me sad. I'm not blaming you but only saying how all this affected me. For instance, I'm proud that Jared and Chad go to camp each summer where they learn new things, meet new kids, and have a chance to grow. It makes me feel good because they are me, and I'm enhanced by their growth and happiness. I regret that I never had the same opportunity and you could not provide those things to me. And you know how I loved sports, spent half my life in the park playing ball. I was a good athlete—very competitive, proud, and hated to lose—all good qualities. I get the same rush now through my kids. I get a kick out of Jared and Chad…watching their personalities in the heat of competition—traits similar to mine. I use sports as a medium to teach your grandkids. I coach them on the town teams, and it gives me a chance to communicate and relate to them beyond just asking if they cleaned their rooms, took the garbage out, or finished their homework. During the week, if there's a game scheduled, they sit at the bottom of the steps in their uniforms holding a ball, waiting for me to come home, so we can have our time winning and losing together."

"I know you are a good father and love those kids, just like I loved you," Mom said.

I heard her but continued my thought. "No one took that kind of interest in me. I didn't have anyone play catch with me or teach me to shoot baskets. I taught myself and played by myself. It hurts me to miss one of the kids' games, and sometimes it's unavoidable, because it is important to them, and they are attempting to please me by doing their best. Parents are required to be there to support and encourage. I recall so many times no one came to see me try to be the best. I would make a good play—shoot a basket or score a touchdown. My teammates and coaches would pat me on my back and congratulate me, but when I looked in the stands, you weren't there to share in my joy, to fill the treasure chest."

"Things were not perfect, and yes, if I could I would have done better by you. I didn't know at the time how harmful some things might have been. I was struggling. Sometimes I think it's my doing. After your father and I broke up, I was still a young woman and hurting from the experience. I know I have passed on and even unintentionally taught you to guard your emotions and intimacy based on a distrust of others and their intentions, because that's how I felt back then. But I hope you are not accusing me of being a bad mother. All the sacrifices I have made—who wiped your diarrhea, stayed up all night with you when you were sick, made the doctor appointments and visits, cooked, cleaned, laughed, and played when I was depressed, and failed to be a wife and mother while I shielded you from my pain? All those sleepless nights waiting for the car to pull into the driveway to let me know you were safe. Goddammit, please don't throw crap in my face...like all the men I knew and gave my best to. It's so funny how I used to think that no matter what happened, I had my baby, and no one could take you away from me."

There was a moment of silence. We had both said a lot. Something interesting was happening to Ma and me. In my opinion, women appreciate these phenomena more than men, when true feelings are exposed through emotional crises such as love, illness, and death. In fact, it may bring out the best of their nature when it happens. Some pejoratively refer to it as drama. I call it pursuit of the truth. More often, mothers and daughters, rather than mothers and sons, make this type of connection. The intimacy and bond, if just temporary from the mutuality of spirit, creates *a touching of the souls*—a thing my mother and I were now experiencing. It opens the portals to the subconscious and brings the unspoken to the surface.

"You know I love you, and God knows you have given me many blessings and proud moments as a parent," Mom said.

"I love you, Mommy. Bear with me. These are troubling times. I appreciate everything you have done for me." My expression of *Mommy* felt warm and was a heartfelt emotion after our time together that afternoon.

"Whatever you do, my son, Mommy is here."

After about two hours, we hugged and kissed, and I left. I think we both felt the long-overdue talk was helpful and necessary. Mom clung to her desire that my situation have a happy ending. On the other hand, I left the same as when I came but was glad that I was able to speak my truth.

I thought about our talk a lot. Pride is an important part of my character. An incident that stands out to this day is as impactful today as it was then. The fourth-grade class at my elementary school was going to Washington, DC, for the class trip. It cost twenty-five dollars to go; everyone had to pay in advance as of a certain date. I brought the information home some two weeks before the due date and was told some time thereafter that I couldn't go because we didn't have the money. In school, the public humiliation was played out when the teacher would ask those few students who hadn't returned their forms and money why and when. I lied and said that I forgot and would bring it next time. This was stressful for a nine-year-old who was popular and the "smartest" boy in the class. Eventually we found the money; we cashed a twenty-five-dollar savings bond I had received at my birthday party when I turned one year old. This recurring pattern of "don't have it" was a consistent theme throughout my youth. When I asked to go with friends to the movies, which cost thirty-five cents, I was always given fifty cents, which meant I had fifteen cents to spend. I had to make a choice between having either a bag of popcorn or a soda, but not both. Again it seemed other kids were luckier than me; they could get popcorn, a soda, and even an ice cream sandwich! If I asked for an additional fifteen cents, I was told, "No, we don't have it." From used bicycles to cheap secondhand clothes, there just wasn't much to be proud of. The hardest part was the loneliness and feeling that nobody really cared or felt I was special…and deserving…nobody willing to sacrifice, share, or compromise for my well-being.

That environment helped define the person I was today. I realized at a very young age that if I was going to reach my potential, I had to rely on myself, my character, and my will and determination. Sometimes it astounds me to think that I had three parents but never received the love, nurturing, and support that I give my kids. Maybe it was meant to be that way. My real father abandoned me when I was two years old. Rachel was a young teenager and overwhelmed with her own failures and much less capable of caring for an infant. The one person I warmly remember is Grandma; she helped raise me. We bonded, and to this day—God bless her soul in heaven—as a result of that early nurturing, we had a special relationship. I remember the two of us being together. I would lie on her stomach while she rested on the couch. I would cuddle against her smooth skin and smell her pleasant scent. I have always had a warm feeling about Grandma, her house, and the sanctuary her home provided.

I thought I should be more empathetic with my mother. She was young and hurt with a new baby, nowhere to turn. I knew she wanted me to be somebody…to prove something to my father and his high and mighty family, who found her undeserving. Maybe in her obsession to prove something and to shield me from the hurt she was feeling, she forgot to hold me close when I needed a hug during those formative years.

I imagined my mother going through the same reflection as me. I envisioned her wrapped in her terry-cloth bathrobe with tears in her eyes. Both sadness and hope sharing space within the same emotional sphere. She probably lay on the couch with her back against the armrest and contemplated her life, our relationship, and her marriages.

CHAPTER TWENTY-ONE

I arrived at work on Monday morning still reeling from the previous week's challenges. I had to focus on my work no matter how distracted I was. I anticipated a meeting with Ted and also wanted to connect with Lawrence to strategize about the Glass-Steagall research and find out from Lawrence about his meeting with the chairman. However, before I did anything, I wanted to see my associate, Ryan.

I dialed Ryan's extension. When he answered, I said, "Ryan, this is Jordan. What happened to you Friday? I missed you at the board presentation."

"Uh, yes…I got pulled away and didn't make it down in time."

"You got pulled away? I had specifically asked you to deliver information on the banking issue. You did understand the importance, didn't you?"

"Yes, sir, I did, and did the best I could, but I had nothing new to contribute. I intend to work on it today."

"Ryan, today is a little late. I had asked you to look into this about weeks ago. Do you know what your lackadaisical attitude cost me? Do you know how I looked and felt when I had no answer for the chairman's question?"

"I apologize."

"If I were in the position to fire you, I would, and I will do my best to see that you don't work on any projects I'm involved in. I need you to bring me all your files, and I will see Ted to have you reassigned immediately. Leave the materials with my secretary, Judy…I need them right away!" Without saying anything more, I slammed the phone down.

"That's done, and I feel good about it. Next I need to see Ted," I thought.

About an hour after my conversation with Ryan, I received a call from Ted's secretary. "Jordan, how are you?"

"Fine, Marsha. I was going to call to set some time up with Ted."

"That's exactly my reason for calling. Can you see him now?"

"Yes, I'll be right over."

Ted was on the phone when I arrived at his corner office, but he motioned me to come in and take a seat. I sat in the cushioned oxblood leather chair facing the front of Ted's cherrywood desk. No less than thirty seconds after I had entered, Ted hung up the phone and turned his attention to me.

"Jordan, how are you?"

"Fine, sir. A little bruised from last week, but alive."

"Your initiation to the board. They are a rambunctious crowd with little patience. I'm sorry you had to experience them the way you did."

"Sir, before you begin, can I express some thoughts I have about the project and give you my take as to why things did not go as planned?"

"Sure. I'd love to hear them," Ted said.

"First, you know that this is not an easy assignment and cuts across a lot of different areas of corporate law. The resources from the beginning were inadequate for the project. Ryan has been a ball and chain around my ankles and is a major reason why I didn't have an adequate response for the banking issue. In fact, I blame him for the failure to respond adequately to the banking issue. I have asked him to return the files and need your support in replacing him on this project. Also, Jim Petrillo, whom I respect and relied on, gave the impression that the issue was a nonissue because the bank's license is dormant, and that project is not on anyone's radar. Finally, sir, I clearly asked Winthrop & Hudson to report on any potential conflicts between this project and others. They assured me of their familiarity with all of Federal's initiative and future plans and said they would cover them in their report. Obviously, this matter was overlooked."

He listened attentively with a blank face, not showing any expression of agreement or disagreement. After I finished, he spoke. "I told you when I hired you that this was a tough culture—and insular. The organization likes homogeneity. The majority is Southern or Midwestern—very conservative—and the higher up you go, the closer the scrutiny. They judge you in terms of your family life, religion, speech, and other things. As large as this company is, it's still run like the mom-and-pop store it started out as in Southern Virginia. It is the face of Jeff Tatum. Nothing gets done without his blessing. That's the culture, this is his game, and that's it."

"Sir, I'm aware of this and realize the roots of the company are Southern, Republican, and evangelical, and New York is not where they prefer to be but are here for business reasons. But I don't see what that has to do with my concerns regarding resources and the professional incompetence of those I relied on...the fact is, there was no one I trust to help get the job done."

"It has everything to do with what I'm about to tell you. I received a call from Chairman Tatum after the presentation, and he blasted me for what happened. He went on about the bank issue and lack of preparedness. He asked why he should have to be the one to do everything with all the people this company employs, and he lashed out at you for wasting the board's time."

Ted paused for a moment and leaned on his desk with his hands clasped. "He asked that another attorney be assigned to the project."

Shocked at the series of statements and accusations, and lacking any rebuttal, I was castrated and made impotent. I shook my head in disbelief and denial. "I think this is unfair. Did you try to convince him otherwise?"

"Given the moment and his anger, there was little I could do. Hopefully, I can speak to him in the future and have a more civil conversation. For now, Jim Stanard will take over. I need you to meet with him right away and get him up to speed. He should also call Lawrence Whitney as soon as possible."

"Should I call Lawrence?"

"No, that would not be a good idea. I'm sorry, Jordan."

"I assume there's nothing more to be said."

"We'll talk later. For now I need you to do what I've asked."

I felt an icy gush of winter chill sweep across the office as if the window opened, and there was a sudden change in forecast, with more bitter weather to come. I got up and walked out of the office to the hallway, headed back to my desk. The reflux action in my stomach was twisting like a wet towel being wrung at opposite ends. It was the same physical reaction I had when I realized Trina was gone.

My legs felt tired and heavy—the air thick, pressing, and asphyxiating as I made my way back to the office. I wanted to hide in the office, close the door, take a deep breath, and resuscitate myself to regain control. The walk through the corridor, which was twenty-five feet from Ted's office, seemed like a mile. I made it, shut the door, and placed my head on the desk, positioning the wastebasket where I could reach it easily if necessary.

It was almost midday, and I assumed word had traveled through the office about the changes Chairman Tatum requested. I had instructed my secretary to hold all calls, and even though the phone rang numerous times, I did not respond and did not know or care who had called. I knew I had to reenter the workplace, so I collected myself and dug deep to pull up strength to face the humiliation and alienation awaiting me on the other side of the door.

"Judy, any messages?" I asked her on the intercom.

"Jim Stanard and Lawrence Whitney called."

"Okay, I'll call them back."

I went to the employee lounge to get coffee and encountered Jim Stanard. He was commiserating with two other attorneys, obviously talking about the recent changes. I could not avoid the head-on collision as they all turned to look at me. Like children caught with their hands in the cookie jar, they looked surprised to see me, stopped in their tracks—probably midsentence—in their recounting of events and opining about the changes and my failings, as well as self-serving justifications for all of it. Typical office gossip that I was as guilty as anyone of engaging in. The satisfaction of this type of banter is that it makes those least affected by the latest execution feel better because they were not the targets.

"Jordan, I called you earlier; we need to talk. Do you have time now?" Jim Standard asked.

The other two attorneys' demeanor abruptly changed. Moments before, they seemed excitedly engaged and clearly speculating and volunteering commentary. Now they acknowledged my presence, quickly finished what they were doing, and left the area.

"I got your message and was collecting materials to bring over. Is this a good time?" I asked.

"Yes, this is good." Not lingering, Jim added milk to his coffee. "I'll see you in my office."

"Be right there as soon as I finish," I said.

A bunch of thoughts ran through my head. I was angry. "I have nothing to be ashamed of, and how dare they judge me! Their opinions do not have value, nor will I allow them credibility as they slow down on the highway to watch a wreck. They have no idea who I am…my strengths and accomplishments. The majority live in their small insular prisms and never step outside their gated communities. One-dimensional men with little penises, who gain their self-esteem through denigrating others…macabre psychotic fascination with other failures…getting pleasure from another's pain, like spectators of Christians' doom in a Roman coliseum. I despise these bastards."

I began the process, as Ted had commanded. Unfortunate and pitiful, I found myself trying to justify to Jim Stanard everything that had happened. It was as if I were speaking to a police officer, trying to reason my way out of a traffic violation. Jim was the least sympathetic person I could talk to. This was a positive development for him. I knew from his facial expressions that he didn't care what the transition represented for me. For Jim, this was a blessing and a career opportunity. He probably figured, "Jordan has done the work, and no one will remember that. Once I go back to the board and repeat everything Jordan had told them and deal with the banking issue, I'll be the hero, and the coffee-area discussion will be about my brilliance and how I pulled this project back from the brink of disaster."

"Patronizing bastard," I thought as I headed back to my office, seething with anger. I was belching and had a throbbing headache. I closed the door to gain sanctuary…and think. "Fuck Lawrence. Let Jim call that soulless weasel bastard; they can all be together in their den, huddling and climbing over one another as Chairman Tatum, the voyeur, watches, and the board strokes him as the orchestra plays a symphony."

I needed to be comforted and couldn't understand why Maria hadn't called. She always called first thing on Monday mornings. I had tried to call her the day before, and she still had not returned my calls. I needed to see her and tried again at her job. She answered.

"Hi, baby," I said. "I needed to hear your voice, and you didn't call this morning."

"Oh," she said, with none of the heightened expression I was accustomed to.

"Is this a good time? Can you talk?" I asked, sensing a less-than-enthusiastic tone.

"Yes, honey. I'm sorry, just caught up in the day...you know how it is."

"Yeah, tell me about it. It has been one of those days over here." Hesitating to get into the details, I left it at that. "What are you doing for lunch? Can we meet? I want to hear about the party and all."

"I'm sorry, baby. If you had called earlier, I could have arranged my schedule, but I have a meeting and planned to get something from the sandwich shop downstairs. I'm sorry."

"What are you doing after work?"

"I can't do that today."

"Why?"

"Jordan, I have things to do after work. Later this week we'll talk."

I sensed a disconnect, something I was unaccustomed to with Maria. I was unable to penetrate the obstruction and decided not to pressure her.

"How was the party?"

"Great! The food, the place, everything. People were dancing and enjoying themselves. I met this film director; he was funny... supposed to produce something later this year. We have to go see it if it comes out. You would have loved it. Stacey had a blast. We danced and ate...I didn't leave until three or four. I missed you not being there. And they surprised me near the end with a beautiful cake, and everyone sang 'Happy Birthday.' It was the best!"

"I figured it would be nice. I'm sorry I couldn't make it. How did people like your jacket and outfit?"

"Baby, it was a hit; everyone liked it. I told them my boyfriend bought it for me. Thank you so much for the gift."

"You don't have to thank me; you deserve it and more. Honey, I need you bad today. Can't I come over?"

"I miss you, too, but I can't see you tonight, honey. I really have to take care of some business. We'll talk about it later. I have to go now. Call me later, okay?" Maria said.

It seemed as if she was hiding something and was unable to come up with a reasonable excuse. I let it go at this point, feeling shut out and rejected. I was in an uncomfortable and unfamiliar zone, particularly with Maria, who till now had been there for me. "Why are you acting so distant? Is there something you're not telling me?"

"Stop, Jordan…let it go. We'll talk…ah…I have to go now. Bye."

After she hung up, I sat at my desk, stunned again at the unraveling of things. "What the fuck is going on?" I thought. Rejection and despondence were everywhere I turned. I had to do something, and remaining behind closed doors for the rest of the day was not the answer. The office was suffocating. I felt like an injured car-crash victim on the side of the road with passing cars creating a traffic jam from rubbernecking as the ambulance and police surrounded the scene and were placing the dazed and injured accident victims into the emergency vehicle. It was only three o'clock in the afternoon, but I decided to leave. I packed my briefcase and stopped by my secretary's desk on the way out.

"Judy, I'm leaving. Not feeling well. I don't expect any important calls, but if anyone is looking for me, tell them I'm out of the office and will return messages tomorrow."

"Hope you're feeling better tomorrow."

"I'll call in the morning if it gets worse. Flu bug is going around…maybe just one of those twenty-four-hour things…I'll call in the tomorrow if I'm not coming in."

"Okay. Feel better. Bye."

I left and on the way out passed Jim Stanard's office. I looked through a glass panel and saw Ryan Douglas laughing with Jim behind the closed door.

CHAPTER TWENTY-TWO

I took a deep breath as I exited the elevator and made my way out of the building onto Seventh Avenue and Broadway. I had no idea where I was headed or what I was doing, but I needed to escape and get a grip on things. After a few blocks, I went down a flight of stairs below ground and entered a local bar and grill. The air was heavy and laden with the stale smell of smoke from thousands of cigarettes exhaled into its windowless hull.

"What can I get for you?" the waiter asked.

"Bombay double with tonic...light on the ice."

The place was empty except for a couple at a candle-lit corner table—obviously romantically involved, holding hands across the table, and engaged in a mating ritual. She would flick her hair on cue; he would pull back on occasion after leaning forward and stick his chest out. She, in turn, would arch her back to display her assets underneath a form-fitting buttoned blouse. They were gaming each other, and the juices were flowing like a brook's water trickling over a slight incline after a spring downpour.

Their actions made me envious and wanting. "How dare she refuse me when I need her, after all I've done for her. Thankless bitch," I thought. I wanted Maria, and that was it. I got up, put money in the payphone, and called her office.

The phone rang five times and switched over to her voice mail.

"Maria, I left my office. Some things went down today. I couldn't talk earlier, but it's not good. That's why I wanted to see you…I'm really feeling bad at the moment. Call me at five-five-five-one-two-three-four. I'm at a bar having a drink. If you can get out for a minute, that would be good. I'll wait to hear from you. Bye."

I returned to the bar and gathered my drink. "Any nuts or chips?" I asked.

"Sure thing," the bartender said from the other side of the bar counter.

I was alone in the dimly lit bar drinking my second double gin. The amorous couple had left, probably to continue their tryst in the privacy of a hotel. Thinking about it made me horny. "Shit! Why hasn't Maria called back? It's almost five o'clock," I thought. I called her again; this time the phone switched over to the receptionist.

"Maria Velez at extension two-five-six-seven," I said.

"She's gone for the day," the woman said.

"Are you sure?"

"Yes, she just left, and the system kicks over to the switchboard at five. Is there a message, or would you like to go to her voice mail?"

"No message. I'll call back tomorrow."

"Fuckin' shittt! What is happening?" I wondered. "Damn! Should I try to catch her? Where is she? If I run over to Sixth and Forty-Fourth, I might be able to intercept her on the way to the subway, assuming she is headed home. Or, if not, I'll just go to her place and wait."

"You okay?" the bartender asked.

"Yeah, I'm fine. How much do I owe you?"

I paid the bill, grabbed my briefcase, and began walking toward Maria's office. Part of the way there, I figured it was useless, and she was gone to wherever by now. I changed directions and headed down Seventh toward the peepshows in Times Square I passed through on occasion, voyeuristically checking out the girls in the booths. I knew the girls changed over at six o'clock, and if I hurried, I could catch this one girl who caught my attention last time I visited. The place was packed with a diverse mix—businessmen passing through before catching their bus or train to the quiet suburbs and dinner with family, as well as an assortment of deviant perverts and others. It was a collection of New York's sexual neediest. The scent was similar to the inside of a car after a car wash when its owner had purchased one of those sweet-smelling deodorizers that hang over the rearview mirror. I looked around to see if the girl I had seen before was there.

"Hey, handsome, you want to come see me?" asked a full-figured vixen in a red wig and a very tiny bikini, her breasts pouring out like foam over a full glass of draft beer.

"No, baby, not now. But let me ask you...do you know this girl—she has black hair about shoulder-length, wears bangs, cute, tall... hair is the same color as her skin. Have you seen her?"

"You mean Toy, the long-legged, dark-skinned sista?"

"Yeah, that's her."

"Oh, you like Toy. That's my girl. She over there," she said, pointing to a booth with the door closed and red light illuminated above it, indicating activity inside.

"Why don't you let me talk to you while you waitin' on my girl? Honey, you know Mama'll take good care of you. Just drop a few coins in the slot and come in...don't be scared...talk to me."

"Next time," I said, smiling at the solicitation and personally feeling wanted for the first time that day. It felt good and complimentary, even if she did it hundreds of times a day. I moved on as she eyed the next prospect and positioned myself near Toy's booth, waiting for her to finish with her customer.

Less than a minute later, the light went out, and a middle-aged white guy, probably an accountant, came from the other end of the booth, hurriedly moving to the exit with his head down and his briefcase in his hand. The girl inside opened the door to the booth, smiling and adjusting the strap to her black lace bra. She looked at me alluringly and said, "Hi. You waiting for me?"

"Yes. You have time? You keep pretty busy, I notice."

"Baby, I can always make time for a handsome brotha like you." She moved closer to me, her breasts inches from my chest.

She seemed much taller than I remembered, with long, sinewy legs jetted up on a pair of fuck-me shoes, high cheekbones, full, painted lips, a small waist, and ample hips and ass painted on a dark canvas of youthful ebony skin.

I started to enter the booth, but Toy stopped me. "Let me call someone over to clean up before you go in. My last friend messed on himself."

"Lucky him," I said.

Toy laughed at the humor of it all and went inside after the cleanup as I entered at the other end. I smelled a faint scent of ammonia and cleaning solvent that slightly irritated my sinuses. Undeterred, I deposited tokens in the slot that gave me a reasonable period of time, probably three minutes or more. Once I deposited the money, the curtain came up, and she stood on the other side of the Plexiglas window next to the stool in her booth. She picked up the receiver on her side.

"I've seen you in here before, but you never come see me."

"Waiting for the right time. Plus, as I said, you're always busy."

"You must be impatient or a busy man; you couldn't wait for me?"

"I waited. Now, I'm here, and good things are supposed to happen to those who wait."

She smiled. "What can I do for you…you want a show?"

"Of course. I like beautiful things."

"Let me put this down," she said, referring to the receiver, "so I can take good care of you. You gonna take care of me?"

"No problem. I can be generous when I'm pleased."

"That's what I like," Toy said as she placed the receiver down and took off her bra. She pressed her breasts against the Plexiglas, expanding the size, contorting the shape, making it seem that her dark areolas covered the entire breast—something my grandfather would have approved of. Her actions elicited an obvious approval from me. I grabbed my crotch, which showed the significant imprint of my dick through my suit pants.

Retrieving the receiver and cradling it on her shoulder, she said, "You gonna show it to me, baby? Let me put it between my tits, and let me suck it." She orally encouraged me as she sat on the stool, her legs spread, the phone between her shoulder and cocked head. She massaged her pussy and tits as she salaciously talked wicked trash. About that time, the curtain started to descend, leaving me feeling like I was in the back seat of a car making out, oblivious to space and time and looking up to see a flashlight shining in my face with an officer asking for identification as the girl scurries to cover up.

"I'm not finished," I said.

"Put some more money in."

I did as she said but dropped in one more token. The curtain came up again, and Toy was still in the same position, waiting for my direction.

"What time do you get off?" I asked, assuming she would be leaving at six.

"Why are you askin'?"

"I'd like to see you after work, outside of here—sit down, talk, have a drink. Whatever you like."

"A date?"

"Call it what you like. Yes, a date…how 'bout it?"

"I don't usually go out with customers, but—"

"Come on. I'm harmless. Just want to do something with you. I like you. I don't usually come here—only once in a while."

"I guess it will be awright. I get off in a few. I have to change. Where do I meet you?"

"Meet me at the Marriott around the corner at the revolving restaurant bar on top. We'll have a drink."

"Sure, I'll come over."

"You promise? Don't have me waiting if you're not coming."

"I said I would. I wouldn't do that…I'll see you there."

"Okay, six thirty. Bye." Before the curtain descended again, I hung up the handset, exited the booth, and left the building feeling nice, for now. The gin and sexy woman made the other events of the day less intense and pressing. "Shit, I didn't tip her," I thought. "What the fuck. I'm seeing her later. Deal with it then."

CHAPTER TWENTY-THREE

I took a window table in the revolving restaurant. It was happy hour, and business types, tourists, and theater-goers occupied the majority of tables. The view of Times Square and other parts of the city was superb, although not as breathtaking as from Windows on the World. The optical omnipotence looking over the valleys of Times Square was spectacular. I could imagine the exhilaration astronauts must feel as they reached the thresholds of space and viewed Earth as a minor part of a large universe subsumed within one of thousands of galaxies and other universes. I ordered another gin and tonic and surveyed the circular revolving room, with its floor-to-ceiling windows for panoramic views and sparkling crystal chandeliers. Across from the windows were mirrored walls with tableclothed banquet tables on which an assortment of hors d'oeuvres, shrimp, patties, fruits, and vegetables was displayed.

About half an hour after my arrival, Toy and the other peepshow girl with the red wig showed up. I saw them first, stood to make myself visible, and motioned with my hand for them to join me.

"There you are!" Toy reacted in an excited voice loud enough to draw the attention of the other patrons. Both girls looked at each other and bent over, pretending to cover their mouths to conceal their raucous laughter at everyone's reaction to their outburst. If the verbal outburst didn't grab you, their appearance surely did. The bountiful, red-wigged peepshow girl was scantily clad in a Superwoman-type outfit consisting of a shiny, black vinyl bustier and pants to match, set off by patent-leather platform stiletto pumps, and an open, fake, reddish-brown fur jacket—best described as exhibitionist style.

In comparison, Toy was relatively toned down, in tight-fitting black jeans tucked inside lavender furry boots and an open, black leather bomber jacket showing a daringly low, V-neck evergreen sweater. Both lugged their signature backpacks that contained the accessories of their day jobs.

"What's happening, girls? That didn't take long."

"It gets crazy with the shift over at six—new girls comin', others tryin' to get out...you have to fight for space in the changing room. Plus, I had to wait for Ebony; she's so slow," said Toy.

"Shuddup, girl. I was waitin' on you...puttin' on all that makeup and shit, tryin' to look good for your man."

"Look who's talkin'. You use a tube of lipstick on those fat lips... bigger than your ass."

"Wow. My name is Jordan," I said, reintroducing myself to the red-wigged girl.

"Hi. Toy is so rude. I'm Ebony. I see you around sometime."

"Yeah, we met earlier. I come through there to check out the girls on my way home."

"Oh yeah, I remember—you wouldn't come in my booth to see me."

Not knowing what to say, I nodded. "You know how it is. I had my eyes on this one for a while," I said, gesturing with my head to Toy but maintaining eye contact with Ebony.

"Ain't he sweet?" Toy said.

"Where's the waiter? I need a drink," Ebony said loudly.

I caught the waiter's eye, and he came to our table. Toy ordered a Long Island Ice Tea and Ebony a Chivas on the rocks.

"There's food along the wall, help yourself," I said.

"I'm hungry. All I had was McDonald's this afternoon. They got any chicken wings?" Ebony asked.

"I haven't been up there. They may…want me to get it?" I said.

"No, I'll go. They must have some shimp…what you want, girl?" she asked Toy.

"Get me some of everything; I don't care. Whatever they have… I'll eat some of yours."

Ebony got up to check out the buffet, and it seemed that all eyes turned to see the spectacle as she maneuvered around and through tables to get to the buffet table. Once there, after surveying the spread, she turned to Toy and me sitting at the table and yelled across the room, "Toy, they ain't got no chicken wings. You want some shimps and some vegetable thingamajigs?"

Toy placed her index finger over her lips, motioning for Ebony to be quiet, and nodded her head. Ebony reacted as told and turned away to finish gathering the food.

"I didn't know you were bringing your friend."

"She's just here to check you out."

"What do you mean?"

"You got to be careful out here. There are some crazy freaks; they wait for you to leave, follow you home…everything. Times Square attracts all kinds. I can tell you some stories."

"I understand. Trust me; I'm not like that."

"I know. Ebony got somewhere to go. She just gonna get her drink on and probably leave. So where you from?"

"I work in the city but live in Jersey."

"Oh yeah, I live in Jersey."

"Where?"

"Jersey City."

"You take the PATH into the city?"

"Yep, every day. So what you do…you married?

"I'm a lawyer, and yes…why do you ask?"

"Big-time lawyer, huh? Most guys your age is married."

"I'm, ah…I'm separated."

"You still wear your ring," Toy said.

"It's something that happened recently." Changing the conversation, I asked, "What about you? Married?"

"I been there and divorced."

"Damn, you don't look that old. How old are you?"

"How old do I look?"

"I figure twenty-two, -three."

"Twenty-two."

Both Ebony and the waiter arrived at the same time with the drinks and food. Ebony was eating the shrimp as she brought it to the table. The waiter looked her up and down, and she returned the look with a bold and unapologetic stare and then turned to wink at Toy before saying in her best Mae West impersonation, "You a cute young thang. You need to come up and see me some time."

The waiter loved it; he blushed while looking directly down Ebony's bustier and moving backward, almost falling into the lap of a patron sitting at another table, as he asked, "Is there anything more?"

We all cracked up, and Ebony continued her act, moving toward the waiter as if she were going to chase him while shaking her breasts like two Jell-O desserts in cups and beckoning him with her finger. He could not contain himself and smiled ear to ear, continuing to retreat to safety.

"I'll wear that boy out, with his li'l cute self," Ebony said.

"I can't take you anywhere," Toy said.

"Look who's talking. You don't want me to tell ya friend 'bout you."

"Just shut up and drink your drink. And what is this food you brought back? Don't they have anything else?"

"I asked you…they have some Jamaican-pie-lookin' things."

"Why didn't you get that?"

"You git your own, bitch. What I look like, ya maid or somethin'?"

"That's what I mean…nigga can't ever do it right. I got to do it myself," Toy retorted.

"Fuck you, Toy…don't get cute with me. I'm hungry. You walk your ass up there and bring me some more shimps!" Ebony yelled.

"Shimps?…what's *shimps*? It's *sshhrriimmppss*, you dumb bitch."

"Ya Mama…just get me some more, and put some hot sauce on them. Tell my waiter boyfriend to see if there are some hot wings in the kitchen."

I sat back in my chair, not saying a word, and just let the minstrel show play itself out. I saw the banter as gaming between friends, verbal competition, and playing the dozens for the last word of nothingness. Besides, the show was entertaining, even if the other patrons didn't appreciate it. I was half-baked like a pound cake in an oven, not yet done but almost ready. I had had four drinks, counting the doubles earlier. Naturally self-conscious, my inhibitions and guarded public persona lessened the more I drank.

The conversation continued for some time thereafter but became more civil as we discussed personal experiences, joked, and sprinkled sexual innuendos throughout the time we were there. Eventually, after a second drink and having gotten her waiter friend to bring her some more shrimp, Ebony received a page, checked the number, and decided it was time for her to leave.

"Well, girl, I gotta go. Meetin' a friend uptown at the Red Rooster…you know what I mean. You okay?" she asked Toy.

"Yeah, I know. I'm fine. See you tomorrow."

I listened but had no clue what the coded messages meant.

"You take care of my girl," Ebony said as she picked up her over-loaded backpack and made her exit with as much fanfare as her entrance. The wives of the gawking middle-aged tourists engaged in an undertone of judgment regarding the conduct and attire of the crass interlopers.

"Your friend is fun crazy."

"That's my homegirl. Her and me have been through a lot to-gether...she's cool. She's my daughter's godmother."

"You have a child?"

"Yeah, a little girl. She's six...stays with my mom during the week and some weekends when I'm busy."

"I have two boys."

My head was expanding with the drinks, and Toy had loosened up. She received a number of pages during the two hours we were sitting there and had gone to the payphone to call back.

Curious, I asked, "What are the pages about?"

"Just my service calling."

"You on call?"

"Yeah, you could say that. I work with a dating service. They want to know my availability, and there are some clients who want to see me...you know. That's why Ebony had to go; she had a date."

I thought, "Escort service?" I didn't ask the follow-up question, deciding discretion was better. Plus, I was enjoying her company, and she seemed to be enjoying mine—why mess it up with details?

"You want to go somewhere else?" I asked.

"You taking me home?"

"Yeah, I said I would. We have to take a train from Penn Station and get my car. You ready to go?"

"Yeah."

Toy lived off Jackson Avenue in Jersey City in a multifamily brick tenement. After inserting her key and opening the front door, having told me she didn't usually bring men home, she invited me up. Once inside she told me, "Hold my bags. I need to stop by and get something from my friend," pointing to an apartment on the first floor. She rang the bell, and someone opened the door. I continued to stand in the corridor near the steps.

"Hey, baby," I overheard a deep baritone voice say from inside the apartment as she stepped inside.

I was feeling lightheaded and down. Since we left the Marriott, half-baked had gone to well done and was now overcooked. Liquor reverses itself—acts as an upper initially and eventually becomes a downer. That was how I was feeling. I took a seat on the stairway, waiting for Toy to return. I leaned back for a minute and must have momentarily dozed off. The next thing I remember was Toy kicking my foot with her boots.

"What's wrong with you, man? Can't hang out...you not fading on me?"

I was startled and drunk but tried to compose myself and said, "No, baby, just taking a time-out. How long you been gone?"

"Just a minute."

"Amazing," I thought. I knew Toy had drunk at least two Long Island Ice Teas and had nodded off during the car ride to her apartment, but now she was moving as if it were the beginning of the day. Her eyes under the green contacts were fiery wide and intense.

"Come on, man...get up. Let's go."

"Where did you go?"

"I had to get something from my friend."

"What?"

"Nuttin'. Come on, if you comin'."

I followed her upstairs, questions unanswered, but realized it was not the time to cross-examine Toy, since she seemed intent on deception. Once inside, she turned on the lights, and I reacted immediately to the clutter and disarray. Clothes were strewn over the room, covering a futon couch; a frayed, flower-patterned upholstered armchair; and a secondhand coffee table covered with mail, papers, and sundry other items. Next to the armchair seat was a TV table that supported an unattractive lamp with a crooked shade and tattered, dangling lining. The lamp offered the only light for the room. In a far corner were cardboard boxes piled on top of one another. It was also extremely hot; the radiator was spitting in concert with the clanking of the heating pipes.

"Put those down," she said, referring to the bags I was carrying. She picked up some of her clothing, particularly the more intimate items—bras, panties, and hosiery—as she took them to the back bedroom. Toy continued to talk as she moved quickly among the three rooms, turning on lights, turning on the radio, and gathering things.

"I just moved in here last month. Don't worry about all the stuff; I'm still unpacking."

Feeling uncomfortable but trying not to show it, I acted as if it was a normal living standard. "Don't worry about it; I know how it is. My place is a mess since things changed. I don't have the time to clean."

"Same here...I'm never home; just come in to sleep, and then I'm gone. I got to call my service. You want something to drink? I got some soda in the fridge."

"I'll have some water—try to clear my head."

"I got something for that," Toy said. I noticed her fidgeting and jerky hand motions; she was moving like a caged animal.

"Oh? What might that be?"

"You so cute and polite, talkin' like a white boy and shit...let me make my calls," Toy said and walked to the phone in the bedroom.

After washing a glass, I got the glass of water from the faucet that she never got for me and made myself as comfortable as possible. I made a space on the futon by moving her dirty clothes to the other side and tried to relax in a strange place.

After she finished her business, Toy called out to me from the bedroom. "Come back here, baby, and talk to me."

"Okay," I said and went to the bedroom.

Toy was on the far side of the bed, sitting on the edge of the queen-sized poster bed that was too large for the room and left little space for anything else. The room was in more disorder than the front room, with too much furniture for the size of the bedroom. She had a large dresser and mirror and two nightstands of Spanish motif and formal lamps with Cupid-like figurines holding the shades of the lamps like opened umbrellas during a rain. Over the bed was a colorful, framed velvet portrait of a naked female with a huge Afro hairdo lying on her side; etched at the bottom of the picture was the caption "Nubian Princess." Nothing matched—it was an eclectic mix of discount and secondhand pieces. Reminded me of furniture in a discount motel—packed wood furniture with fake veneer. On one side of the room was a cot with rumpled sheets and covers. I assumed her daughter must sleep there. She had her back to me as I entered the room and was furtively unwrapping a package and placing the contents of brownish rocks in a glass pipe and beginning to light it with a Bic lighter.

I realized now exactly what all the previous subterfuge was about. Toy had purchased crack cocaine from the apartment downstairs and obviously had tried the product while there, which explained the intense eyes and herky-jerky motions I noticed earlier.

Inhaling a lavish amount into her lungs, she offered me the same. I had sniffed a fair amount of coke over the years but never smoked crack. The first thing that crossed my mind was the politics of criminal justice and the disproportionate sentencing and convictions with the racial overtones for powdered coke versus crack. I drew the substance into my body as I lit the pipe. Toy looked on with a devilish smile. My lungs filled up as I lost my virginity.

Instantly, I experienced a strange reaction; every electrolyte in my body sparkled like a Fourth of July flare, setting in motion an intense surge of energy. I could feel my blood rushing through my veins and hear my heart pound against the rib cage. At that moment, nothing else mattered. The cerebral focus of attention was a feeling of ecstasy with undeniable gemstone clarity. This was a complete reversal of the depression I had from the day's events. The crack easily overtook the gin and tonics I drank. My body reacted to the bolt of lightning, and I began coughing. I handed the pipe back to Toy.

"You awright, baby doll?" she said as she patted me gently on the back, taking the pipe with her other hand.

"Wooww, that is powerful stuff," I said, rising up from my position on the bed.

"You like that...I told you I would take care of you...feel better now. Look at your eyes, nigga. They are 'bout to pop outta ya head."

"Come here, baby, let me hold you," I said.

"Whatcha want, Daddy?" she said, moving into my arms as we stood. I grabbed her waist and pulled her tighter with no resistance.

No words were spoken at this point, and the foreplay earlier at the peepshow, the crack, the drinks, the stress of work, the family breakup, and the MIA mistress all gushed forward at that moment like a geyser in a national park. I was angry and felt violent with pornographic urges; my kiss reflected those urges. Toy opened her mouth to accept my tides, and she sensed my passion and acted as passionately. She recognized my needs and was as just as angry as I was, if not angrier. A single parent living on the fringes as an outlier trying to make it day to day with no reliable support—low self-esteem...hopelessness...jerking off men in booths for tips...fondled and fucked by strangers for money...helplessly fucked by everyone who ever entered her life until she decided to fuck them back.

Without hesitating, Toy unbuckled my pants, letting them drop to the floor. She slid my underwear down and with aggressive urgency sought to get my dick in her mouth. Like a newborn sucking a taut nipple, she began an up-and-down motion on the stem, massaging with her tongue, jaw muscles, and inner crevices of her mouth—the indentations in her cheeks pronounced and pulsating. My length and girth were total, the compound effect of blood filling my outer vessels, semen percolating, and increased ecstasy. Toy was experiencing my heightened sensitivity, which in turn, elevated her pleasure. She seemed to enjoy sucking cock as much as I enjoyed receiving the pleasure. Her mouth was wet and moist, her saliva increasing with each stroke.

I had abandoned all caution and was overwhelmed with nature's most powerful urge. AIDS, STDs, disease—nothing presented a conscious barrier to my nature. Besides, she was not Haitian, an IV-drug user, or homosexual. Like a lab rat that chooses an addictive drug over food and eventually dies of starvation—I blew caution to the wind.

Toy conducted the symphony and removed her sweater top and pants. Her pussy was dilated and contracted, vagina lips becoming more sensitized and swollen as nature's lubricant flowed like a river into the area. Completely naked, she lay on her back, and I straddled her youthful, taut body. She grabbed my penis and began massaging it with her hand, momentarily pausing to place some body lotion in her hand to reduce the friction and create a sensation of a moist vagina. I resisted the power of her act so not to cum prematurely. Feeling the urges building, I took charge and straddled her as she lay on her back with her legs splayed open. She reached down as I fondled her tits and guided my cock by gently holding my balls while inserting the circumcised head into her entrance. She pulled it out after one or two inches of depth, maneuvering it up to stroke her clit and vagina lips.

"You like that, Daddy? Easy, baby, just like that, baby," she murmured as she manipulated me like a dildo. We explored and uncovered pleasing sensations, changing up and repeating with more intensity the longer we engaged.

I wanted to be completely inside and was beside myself. I grabbed her hands, placing them over her head, and held them in a bondage position as I inserted deep inside her pussy.

"Oohh yes...oh yes, that's it," Toy said.

"You like that, baby...is it good?" I said while alternating between kissing her mouth and sucking her nipples as I continued to penetrate her.

"Oh yeeah, fuck it...shove that big dick in my pussy, baby. You like Mommy's pussy."

I was out of control; the language and uninhibited aggressiveness were dirty, savage, and gritty. She was touching the deep recesses of my primal manhood. She was only beginning and wanted more as I violently pumped and thrust my pistonlike dick in her.

Then she whispered, "Turn me over; I want you in my ass."

I have never felt so virile, and in the crossfire of guilt related to the extremity of her actions and the pleasure of it all, my mind quickly dismissed guilt for pleasure. I entered the most forbidden and nasty orifice of her body—the anus—where waste, decay, and excretion exit. I easily crossed this moral threshold and demarcation and entered her from the back, dipping my penis into her ass. She was perched doggie-style, ass up, and receptive without lubrication but for the juices that flowed from her pussy that were on my dick. She was tight and opened up to envelop my member.

"Stoke my ass, you mothafucka. I want to feel your hot cum in my ass!" Toy screamed, her voice and movements uncontrollable. "Pleeaassee, baby, hurt this fuckin' pussy." And I tried my best, finally giving way to the uncontrollably strong force of nature. I unloaded a cargo of fluid into her body. Moments before the delivery, I felt her expand to accept my load.

"Oohh, shit, baby, fuck meee!" I screamed at the moment of climax.

After the deposit, some fluid oozed outside her orifice and trickled out her ass and down her thigh. I rested on my knees behind her, looking down while holding my semierect, still-throbbing dick. She turned over, propped herself up on her back with a pillow, and held her legs wide and high off the mattress, as if in doctor's-office stirrups. She peered between her trembling legs, spreading her pussy with her hands as she arched her back, and as if pushing a newborn during birth, squirted a fine mist of cum from between her legs as she screamed in orgasmic satisfaction. The mist settled on my stomach and lower chest as I faced her.

"Ahhh, shit, that was good, sugar...you so nasty," she said, eyes rolling back in her head. She turned to a fetal position, and I assumed a position lying next to her. We were comatose, our nerves relaxed and at rest, oblivious to the collective lemony mixture of perspiration and sexual fluids we were lying in.

"It was all you; I'm just here."

"Shuddup, nigga, you tried to kill me."

"What was that squirt thing? I never had that done to me before," I asked, having read about female ejaculation but having never experienced it.

"Just a little something special, baby...you enjoy?"

"Yeah, just—"

"Just what? Don't think so much. Enjoy and relax...it is what it is."

"Okay. I hear you."

"You want another hit?" Toy asked, referring to the rocks she placed in the pipe.

"Sure." Taking the pipe from her, I lit it like a professional, and we shared as we had done previously. We repeated the cycle until exhausted and then retreated to opposite sides of the bed from uselessness, having depleted each other's energy—finally falling asleep.

CHAPTER TWENTY-FOUR

My binge lasted longer than I had anticipated. The next afternoon, the drug-induced lovefest started to wane as ecstasy gave way to irritability when the supply was exhausted. At one point I was on my knees parsing through grit and lint in the carpet, trying to uncover a renegade piece of rock that may have fallen to the floor.

"How much you wanna get?" Toy asked.

"Tell me," I said.

"You want an eight ball?"

I was clueless to the street-drug vernacular and how much or what an eight ball was. "Yeah, that should be enough. How much you need?"

"Let me have two hundred, baby," Toy said as she moved to the bathroom and talked over the running water while she washed her face and lower body.

"How much is that?"

"I told you two hundred!"

"I mean weight."

"You know…about an eighth ounce; you said get an eight ball, right?" Toy sounded irritated about having to keep repeating herself.

"Why don't we get half that amount for now? I'll buy more later. Are you hungry? We haven't eaten since yesterday." I figured an eighth of an ounce was probably too much.

"Okay, I'll get five or six rocks. He'll probably throw more in for me. Gimme a C-note, and get me a Big Mac, fries, and Coke…the McDonald's is down the street about two blocks."

"Do they deliver?" I said jokingly, rolling over under the covers of the unmade bed that didn't faze me any longer.

"Get up, sweetie, and feed me. Go on, now, while I go downstairs."

I got up, went into the bathroom, and called out while sitting on the toilet, "I need a washcloth and towel." My body felt like it had been in a prizefight.

"Here," she said, handing me a towel and washcloth through a partially open door. "You want me to wait for you?"

"Yeah, I'll be right there. I'm just washing up."

"Hurry up."

We left the apartment together. I handed Toy a hundred dollars and went on a hunt for food while she went to gather more crack. I got the fast food and withdrew money from an ATM before returning. When I arrived, Toy was on the phone talking.

"Tomorrow is fine. Six thirty at Belagio on Fifty-Eighth between Second and Third…okay, fine. Bye."

I realized I had not called my job that morning, not that I could have, even if I remembered, but my sense of responsibility was acute, and I wondered what to do. I thought, "I'll call tomorrow morning. I told Judy I might not be in, and she probably figured I was sick. I'll check my messages at home later."

"Good. I got a job tomorrow night. You know Charly D, the radio DJ?"

"Yeah…why?"

"I'm meeting him for drinks, and he wants to go clubbing after."

"This is your dating service?"

"Girl got to pay the rent, which reminds me. You know my baby needs milk, and Mama needs a new pair of shoes. You gonna give me a li'l sometin' before you leave?"

I knew from her tone and look that Toy was not asking but telling me this was not a free ride. I was not completely naïve and didn't have a problem paying for her sex, particularly the way Toy dealt with customer service. Some Fortune 100 companies could learn from her.

"Oh yeah…sure, baby. I'll…give you something for shoes and milk. You want it now?"

"No, we got time…tomorrow's fine. I need about three hundred to buy some things for my apartment…okay, sugar? I'm sure you pay more to your wife, and she probably don't fuck you like I do, baby. You know what I'm sayin'?"

Not knowing where she was going with this and noticing a character reversal and detecting sarcasm and meanness in her tone of voice, I backed off, not wanting to aggravate her and have her go off on me.

"Sure. Slow down," I said. "I told you I'm a giver, and I like you. Let's be easy, get high, make love…I'll be going in the morning… you're not mad, are you?"

"No. But you know how it is out here. Niggas take, talk shit, and make promises they can't keep and leave you with worthless promises that can't be cashed. Don't offer me promises and lies; just leave the Benjamins in the kitty and call me next time…latteerr," she said, raising her hand and cutting it through the air like a sword as she snapped her finger.

"I understand, trust me. I'm not looking to take from you. We okay?"

"Sure." She unwrapped her burger and began sipping the soda through a straw.

I left the next morning, after two days, to go home. I gave Toy three hundred dollars. We exchanged numbers; she gave me her pager number, and I left my business card. I wanted to maintain the supply chain and left with a few rocks from the last purchase. My head was misty from the romp, but the haze was starting to give way to reality—my problems seemed compounded. When I reached my car, the sight added to my woes. It had been broken into. The passenger-side window had been smashed, and glass was spread all over the sidewalk.

"Shit, I just got this out of the shop," I said out loud. Once inside, I found that my radio had been ripped out of the console and loose change taken from the ashtray. To add insult to injury, there was a ticket for overtime parking on the windshield.

CHAPTER TWENTY-FIVE

I t had been three weeks since the reassignment and time spent
with Toy and close to a month since Trina and the boys had left.
It felt longer—I missed her and the boys. I spoke to the kids on the
phone to see how things were. We went to the movies one weekend,
but it was strange and unsettling to be separated. Trina had a new
job with a public relations firm and was going through orientation
and meeting with clients. Her job was new-business development
and required considerable social and political networking. I hated
the loneliness of an empty house.

I avoided the people at work as much as possible. I was ex-
cluded from meetings and concentrated on some small projects. I
stayed late at work to fill the voids in my life. I was depressed—not
clinically—but needed help. My behavior was erratic, and I was
self-medicating at nights, when it was most severe, smoking and
drinking until I passed out.

It was clear Maria was avoiding me; I had not seen her since
the party. We talked, and she said her workload was the problem. I
was suspicious but had nothing to validate my concern. I knew she

was out of town on business for the last two weeks, and we planned to see each other this week. I was anxious to reconnect and spend time with her.

It was early evening, and I had to talk to my boys. I hated calling Hazel's house and asking to speak to Chad and Jared. I always resented the fact that Hazel might answer, and I would have to go through her to get to my kids. As always, I called in spite of the reluctance. Hazel would not stop me from speaking to my children and her daughter.

After about four rings, this clear, innocent voice that pierced my heart said, "Hello, who's calling?"

"It's Dad. *¿Que pasa*, man?"

"K what?"

"*¿Que pasa*—it's Spanish for what's happening. How are you doing?"

"Hi, Daddy. I'm doing fine. Are you coming home?"

"You mean to your grandma's? No, not tonight. I'm at our house."

"I want to go home with you."

"Not tonight, buddy. I'll have to talk to Mommy about when you guys are coming home."

"Who's that?" I heard Trina say from another room in the house.

"It's Daddy, Mommy."

"How's Jared?" I asked Chad.

"Good," Chad responded.

"What's he doing?"

"Watchin' TV."

"Well, let me speak to your mother and see what she's doin'. You be good, and maybe you guys can come see me this weekend. I'll talk to your mom, okay?"

"Okay, Daddy, I'll see you later."

"See ya, and I love you," I said as the brief conversation ended.

"Mommy, it's Daddy!" Chad yelled.

After a moment, Trina picked up the phone and said, "Hi, Jordan. How are you?"

"I'm fine. How 'bout you?"

"Tired, stressed, not enough sleep. New job and all."

"I'm happy for you; I'm sure they love you. Once you get acclimated, things will fall into place."

"We'll see. Right now, it's tough. And what about your situation? You didn't get into the details, but said you were going through a rough patch after the presentation you worked so hard on."

"That's another story and one of the things I want to talk about, besides us and the boys. How are the boys doing? Chad says he wants to come home. I want you and the boys to come home."

"Jordan, stop. You can't just play with people's emotions like a yo-yo. What are you saying?"

"I want us to talk, to sit down, and try to work things out, to put the family first."

"I've always put the family first. I don't think that is an issue for me. The question is your priorities."

"We have a lot to talk about. I want you back and for us to talk about you coming home."

"We'll talk when I'm ready. I'll let you know—not now," Trina said.

"Okay. You promise? Remember the boys are spending the day this Saturday."

"I know. I'll drop them off in the afternoon."

"Good. I'll see you then. Let me yell at Jared."

"Jared, come to the phone. I'll see you Saturday, Jordan…bye," Trina said.

Jared answered the phone with "Hello."

"Hey, little man. How you doin'?"

"I'm fine."

"You watchin' television? What's on?"

"Cartoons. Daddy, Chad won't let me play with his video game."

"Why not?"

"I don't know."

"You tell him I said let you play. Those games are for both of you, and he should share and teach you. Okay?"

"Yep." Before I could say another word, he dropped the phone, and I could hear him yelling at Chad, "Daddy said let me play with the video games, now!"

Trina picked up the phone and said, "What did you tell that boy? He's going crazy."

"I just told him he could play with the video games. What's the big deal? They both play, don't they?"

"Yes, they play, but you know how territorial they get—'This is mine'—Chad is afraid Jared will break something. Jared is too young for some games. It goes on and on. Another thing I've been meaning to say is you need talk to your son. Chad's been asking a lot of questions. We can't keep avoiding them."

"We'll spend time this Saturday, and I'll see what he's thinking."

"Well, see you then. Bye," Trina said as she hung up.

I was better after speaking to Trina and the kids; it briefly rejuvenated me. The separation hurt but made me realize how much I needed them. The pleasure and involvement with Maria made me misplace those feelings. Occasionally I thought of family as an obstacle to my relationship with Maria. Things were not resolved, and the two emotions were still pitted against one another. The prospect of losing either or everything was disturbing.

CHAPTER TWENTY-SIX

The day after speaking with Trina, I decided to surprise Maria for lunch; I knew she was back from her business trips. I sat in the front of her building on the granite seating facade near the building's water fountain twenty feet from the front entrance and watched the comings and goings of everyone who worked or had business affairs there. I knew her schedule—she normally went to lunch around one, and I expected her to show shortly. My hunch was almost correct. At about twelve forty-five, she came out with another woman, and they turned left along the building's perimeter and walked to where I was sitting.

"Maria," I said, getting up from my seat and moving toward her.

She turned her head in response to my voice and looked startled, like a doe caught in the headlights of an oncoming car on a deserted rural road. The startled look was quickly replaced with a stare that conveyed distress.

"Hi, Jordan. Surprise…what's going on, honey?" she said as she and her companion's way was now blocked by my intrusion.

"I'm fine. I was in the area…thought I might run into you," I said, trying to sound casual and nonchalant for the benefit of Maria's business acquaintance.

"Jordan, this is Cathy…Cathy, Jordan Baros."

"Hi, Cathy," I said, extending my hand to shake hers.

"We were headed to the Korean place down the street to grab a salad or something."

Having satisfied protocol, I became more assertive. "I wanted to talk to you. I have been calling you…think we can meet? It's fairly important."

"Sure, that's fine." Turning to Cathy, Maria said, "You don't mind, do you? I need to talk to Jordan. Will you be okay? I'm sorry."

"No problem. I'll just get my food and run back to my desk…it's fine, no big deal. Nice meeting you," Cathy said as she walked away.

"So why haven't you called, or what is the avoidance all about?" I asked.

"I've been busy. Like I told you, I was away on business the last two weeks. This is my first time in the office, and I've been waiting for the right time."

"I don't understand…the right time for what?"

"Can we go sit down? I don't want to stand here talking."

"Whatever you want to do. Where you wanna go?"

"Just around the corner; we can sit down at the café there."

Once inside the café, we took a seat away from the front window along a wall and ordered lunch. Maria ordered soup and salad, and I got a chicken salad on a croissant.

"You look tired," she said.

"I'm under a lot of pressure at work."

"I can tell by your eyes, the dark circles. Looks like you haven't slept, and you've lost more weight."

"It's been tough lately. I took the rest of the day off. So what's your story? Why are you avoiding me?"

"I'm not avoiding you."

"I haven't seen you in weeks...you don't return my phone calls... when we do talk, you are in a hurry to get off the phone. I'm not stupid; I know the difference. Just be straight with me," I said, my voice rising as I spoke.

"Please, Jordan, keep it down."

"Okay, but talk to me. What's happened since the party...that I need to know about?"

"It's not the party...it's us. What am I supposed to do? Do you ever think about how I feel or what it's been like since we started going out? You can't believe that this is the best thing for me...or do you?"

"What do you mean?"

"I'm talking about me, my life...so-called life. You don't know what it's like to sit around unable to do what you want to do because you're thinking 'bout someone else...obsessed with them, and they're not even reachable. You know what I did Christmas? I fixed dinner for myself, by myself...watched TV...and the high point was your call late that evening that I waited for all day. And you began the call with, 'I can't talk long, but I wanted to wish you a Merry Christmas, and I love you.' And I accepted that as compensation for my pain, loneliness, and self-pity. A fuckin' phone call! Is that all my life is? How was your Christmas? I'm sure much better than mine. How is your life compared to mine? Do you sit around waiting for me to call, Jordan?" Tears welled in her eyes as she looked directly at me.

"You have not suffered alone, Maria...I have lost a lot and given a lot. My family, my kids are gone. I go home to an empty house."

"Welcome to my world. Even now, you say your wife has left, but you haven't come to me. You're still holding on to your cozy little life with Trina, afraid to do anything else. You say you want to be with me, but do you really? Your infatuation is a self-indulgent need to have me, your family, and Trina...everything. This is more about Jordan than anything else, and I'm another trophy in your tournament, to show the world and to convince yourself how great you are or maybe how pitiful and sick you are. I can't be your medication. Your needs are deeper than anything I can offer. My continued relationship with you is at times fulfilling—I don't deny that. But it's also my demise. You are limiting me to serve your own needs. I should have walked away when I had a chance. That day you approached, you knew exactly what you were doing...I have no more to give."

"You think I'm a selfish ingrate? After all we've shared. How can you change that suddenly...just walk away and accuse me of all this. You can't believe that...it's not true, and you know it. I love you and always will. I have made sacrifices to prove it to you. You know how deeply I care. The fact that I have not thrown everything away does not mean I don't care. You can't mean what you're saying. Plus, you are the one with the history of spurned affairs and relationships...men have offered you love and affection, only to be burned when you chose to move on to the next adventure... lover."

"How dare you throw that in my face! You don't know anything about my past. There are things you will never know...things I can't face or explain. I was soiled years ago and have tried to forget and better myself. Can you imagine what it is like to have an alcoholic father? I was a ten-year-old child who had to protect an adult...to put him to bed when he came home at night too drunk to walk. Mom would tell me, 'Daddy's sick,' so I would stay with him, would lie next to him, hoping to make him better. I lay there staring at the ceiling while he would finger my hair, take off my pajamas and fondle me, and tickle my feet under the covers while licking my vagina and bottom. When he finished, he'd stumble into the bathroom, pulling me from behind, and wash the sticky mess he made on me. 'This is our secret,' he told me. I never told a soul."

"I'm so sorry for you," was all I could say. I was shocked, and it made everything else incidental.

"I have a good heart. I gave you that heart, and yes, others have seen it, but not like you. I have not been as lucky as you or Jania. I have always wanted that one person, kids…house to call a home… people who genuinely love and respect me. But I was dealt a different hand, and I accept that. I live my truth and will continue to do so. To answer your question, yes, I met someone at my birthday party. The one you couldn't come to, and hopefully, I will continue to meet someone special who will give back what I can give them."

"Oh, so I was right. I thought something had happened." It was a reflex response.

"Right!? That I met someone who could offer me a whole life, a chance to dream of more and have what you have. Is that so bad? Am I a ho and a bitch for wanting what you take for granted?"

"Maria, I hear everything you're saying and didn't mean what I just said. I just knew something had happened. I don't know what to say about all this. I never intended to hurt you or for us to get to this. I do love you…too much to stand in the way of your dreams… your life and happiness. I'm not selfish and have never been. I understand exactly, and I apologize for not recognizing it sooner. And you're right. I'm trying to hold on…I'm confused and have not left Trina for that very reason."

Removing a handkerchief and compact from her purse, she wiped her eyes and face, which was stained from her tear-soaked mascara. "I have to freshen up. Are you going to eat?" she asked, trying to compose herself. Both lunches were untouched.

"I'll eat what I can; I'll have the waitress pack yours to go."

When Maria returned from the ladies' room, there was a distinct makeover—too much—as she attempted to hide the emotions that had just surfaced. I reached across the table and held her hand in mine. "I'm losing you, and it hurts. You have been my strength. We both carry a lot of resentment and anger, but you can't blame me for what others have done to you—it's not me. I don't know what to do; I have lost everything. It's a desert, and

I'm trying to find an oasis. There is an emptiness that leaves me lifeless."

"Jordan, don't make me cry anymore. You know what you want...maybe this will help you to better appreciate things. You love Trina. I know that, and you were not going to abandon those boys like your father did you. I never meant to be the one to interfere with your family, and now I feel better...that we both have a chance...I have to go now."

"You want me to walk back with you?"

"No, I need to be by myself...bye, Jordan."

The encounter was overwhelming. I sat there alone with the painful answers I finally got to the suspicions I had had for the past weeks. I was engulfed in a numbing emptiness and realization as love drained from my heart, like the feelings at my grandmother's funeral and burial, when they placed her coffin in the ground. It was raining, which mingled with the tears streaming down my face after I left the café, turned the corner, and walked down the street.

CHAPTER TWENTY-SEVEN

In spite of Trina's refusal to start over, I sensed a breakthrough in our estrangement. The anger had subsided, Trina was working, and we were committed to the best interests of our children. I was still recoiling from the shocking breakup with Maria; paradoxically, I turned my attention to my kids and my hope to reclaim Trina's affections. I wanted to begin the healing process.

The plan was for Trina to bring Chad and Jared to the house. She was going to be a panelist at a conference at Rutgers University about women in the professions that afternoon. Trina called around eleven to let me know they were on the way. She arrived some thirty minutes later, and I watched from the living-room window as the family SUV Jeep pulled into the driveway. Chad jumped out first as the car came to a halt and was making his way to the front door when Trina disrupted his progress.

"Slow down, Chad, and wait for your brother."

Obediently he stopped in his tracks and waited for Jared, and together they resumed the approach to the front door to see me. I moved from the living-room window to the front as they were making their way to the house. Before they rang the bell, I had opened the door to greet them.

"Hey, boys, how you guys doing?" I asked cheerfully.

"Hey, Dad," they both responded as I bent down to hug both.

"Where's Mom?"

"She's coming." Before Chad had barely gotten the answer to the question out, Trina walked through the open door wearing an open, full-length navy-blue wool coat, exposing her gray, pin-striped conservative pantsuit and one-inch black business pumps.

We greeted each other like attendees at a business meeting—the only thing missing was the obligatory handshake.

"Hello, Jordan," Trina said with no enthusiasm or warmth in her voice.

"Hi, how are you?"

Without responding to the question, Trina said, "I will be back later this evening, probably around seven. Is that okay?"

"Sure, we'll be here."

"Jared has a little cold. There's some cough syrup upstairs; you know what to do if he starts coughing."

"No problem, Trina," I said, wondering why she was acting as if I was some new babysitter.

"I've got to run, don't want to be late." She leaned over to kiss the boys.

I followed her out the door to the porch. Looking directly at me for the first time, she said as she was leaving, "We need to go out; think about what we're going to do."

Without looking at Trina directly, I mumbled, "I know; you let me know when."

"And remember what I said about Chad. Talk to him about what's going on. He needs his father to talk to him. Jared is too young; he doesn't say anything."

"I will. Don't worry."

Trina got into the car and backed out of the driveway, never looking back. I stood there frozen and did not take my eyes off her until the car turned the corner and was out of sight. For the second time in the past twenty-four hours, I plummeted into emptiness.

Trina returned to the house much later than she had planned. It gave me more time with the boys; we had a good time that day. I made them blueberry pancakes, and we had a pillow fight, played hide-and-seek, and played a game of pile-on knee football in the living room. We went out to fetch some food and cuddled up on the couch under a blanket to watch a pay-per-view *WrestleMania* starring Hulk Hogan. They were exhausted later that evening, and I carried them to their bunk beds, tucked them in, and kissed them both on their foreheads.

Trina eventually returned. I told her about our day and that Chad and I talked. I explained that Chad missed his friends. I told her I had delicately explained that we were taking a break, that we loved him, and not to worry—I would always be there for him.

"He wants us to be a family again," I said to Trina.

She nodded. "It's hard on all of us."

I decided to pursue the line of thought I started earlier. "All I did today was think how much I miss you and the boys. Spilled cereal, boys fighting, getting them to their games, you and I taking a moment on weekends together…I miss that."

"Jordan, I don't know how to take you. Everything you're saying was exactly what you were running away from. Either you are crazy or a liar. What about your girlfriend?"

"That's over. I'm sorry that I lost my way, that you found out the way you did, and that I did it. It was wrong, and I apologize for hurting you and the kids. I'm not crazy or a liar…I'm neither. I'm the same person you've always known. I love you and our family, and I want you back."

Smiling without saying anything, Trina changed the subject. "I met some interesting people today. One woman told me about an exhibit she saw in Chicago that is now in New York. There's an article in today's *Times* about a showing of some of Charles Alston's works at a gallery in SoHo. I thought that might be a good place for us to go."

"Who's Charles Alston?" I asked.

Trina had taken credits in fine-arts courses while at Cornell and was relatively familiar with African American art. "He was a major artist during the post-Harlem Renaissance period and taught and mentored Jacob Lawrence. Some of his works are caricatures of Harlem nightclubbers, civil-rights protest paintings, and depictions of black life. He's also very well known for the huge murals he painted. There's one in Harlem Hospital that traces the development of medicine from chants, superstitions about animals, and dance of African witch doctors to modern scientific discoveries. He did another in the Bronx Family Criminal Court building. You'll enjoy his stuff."

This is what impressed me about Trina—her breadth of knowledge and interest. I had learned so much from her over the years and continued to do so.

"I'd love to go. Let's do that soon?"

"We can do it. This will be good. We haven't done this in a while, a nice afternoon in the Village." Trina seemed excited about the thought.

"Not to be a downer, but you know I'm having a problem at work," I said, making a transition into the other issue that was bothering me.

"How did the presentation go? The one you worked on for months."

My face showed dissatisfaction. "Not as well as I would have liked. I've tried to forget it."

"You're always so self-critical. I'm sure it went well. What did your boss say?"

"We met, and he took me off the project."

"What was the problem? What went wrong?"

"I did a lot of work on this project, and you know from what I told you it was complicated and involved, with securities and broker-dealer laws. Federal wants to set up a money-market fund for its card holders and insurance customers...to try to capture some of its retail customers' money through another vehicle."

"Yes, you told me...sounds complicated, I know. But you said you had outside counsel and all, and everything was going well."

"Yeah, well, that's true, and I did a bang-up job researching and assigning tasks, even with limited support. I never had the right resources for what the project required. They assigned this jerk young attorney, who I had to follow up with every minute. The businesspeople I needed information from were always too busy and either gave me half-ass feedback or nothing at all. Ted, my boss, Mister Reverse Discrimination, left me out there by myself. And that's the point: People didn't respond to my requests. I tried to do it all, which is impossible, and with everything involved, something was bound to get dropped—Murphy's Law. And I'm the fall guy, the black attorney...who didn't do his job. Stereotypical shit. I'm out there, as usual, trying to prove something, and everyone sits back waiting for me to fail. It's a self-fulfilling prophecy."

"What happened?"

"Everything was going well; they loved it. And then the chairman raised an issue about a bank Federal bought about three years ago and the impact that deal would have on this one. That's when everyone ran for cover and left me to fend for myself. I don't mind that, but with everything else going on, I had asked no fewer than three people to address the bank issue, including five-hundred-bucks-an-hour outside counsel, and no one did anything. So I look like a jerk."

"Didn't you tell them you asked outside counsel to look into it?"

"How could I? Anyway, he sat next to me at the table and said he was never asked the question. Besides, I couldn't sit in that meeting and start blaming everyone else. Plus, they don't care. Their issue is blame and responsibility. Outside counsel's been around for ages, and his father before him. I've been there two years, the only black attorney on staff, the first they've ever hired."

"You think it was racism?"

"Race is always a factor; you know that. I don't get the pass others do. That's why I'm upset. When I first started there, I wrote a legal memo to one of the vice presidents, arguing the merits of a transaction. He praised the quality of the work and then challenged its authenticity by questioning me about who had written it, even suggesting that a white intern who had helped with the research was the author. Who knows? They may fire me."

"Don't say that. You gave them a lot; you just have to resolve one last issue. Stop beating yourself up. You're a good lawyer—smart and competent...they know that, I'm sure."

"That's good to hear, but you don't know what it's like."

"I do know. I'm dealing with the same thing at my job."

"You have always had confidence in me, even when I didn't have it in myself. You're the one person who has seen it all and never second-guessed my ability or lost faith."

Not saying anything, Trina exuded warmth. We were connecting more than we had in a while. We spoke as a couple, not separate individuals sharing common space, which had been the case for too long. I was sharing my pain, and she showed compassion.

I asked her to let the boys stay, but she wanted to take them to church in the morning. I didn't object. We woke them up and put them in warm clothing, and I carried each to the car. When I placed Chad in the car, he looked at both of us and said, "Why can't I stay home, Mommy? I don't want to go to Grandma's."

Trina and I both looked inquisitively at each other, trying to decide who was going to answer the question and how to answer it. Avoiding the substance of the question, Trina judiciously said, "You are spending the night at your grandmother's with your brother. We have to go to church in the morning."

CHAPTER TWENTY-EIGHT

The week started out as usual. I called in early and left a voice message saying I wasn't feeling well but would be in later. I got to the city about twelve and had a liquid lunch to brace myself. I thought about calling Maria but decided not to; instead, I called the job again, undecided if I would go in or not.

"Hi, Judy. Do I have any messages?"

"How are you?"

"I'm doing better. I'll be there shortly; just wanted to recheck on things before I get there."

"Glad to hear that. Ted stopped by and just asked how you were. I'll let him know you'll be in."

"Yes, I'll be there, next hour."

"A Ms. Toy called. She was very rude and didn't leave a message. Who is she?"

"Huh? Oh, I...ah...do some work outside the office, small things, people refer them to me...you know. I'm handling a car-accident case of hers. She's probably upset over that. I'll talk to her. Did she leave a number?"

"No, she said you had it. Other than that, Jim Stanard was looking for you earlier. I told him you were out sick. He didn't act as if it was urgent."

"Good. I'll see you in a little bit."

"Damn, what does Toy want?" I wondered. "Why did she call my job and draw attention to herself? That's my job. Why did I give her that number? She's such a stupid bitch. I need to call her to get some stuff to get high." I had the number to the peepshow and figured she might be there.

"Hello, hello. Can you hear me?" Loud music was playing in the background.

"Hi. Who's this?" a gruff male voice on the other end said.

"Is Toy there? I need to talk with her."

"She's working, gets off at six."

"This is an emergency, and she said to call here. Tell her Jordan is calling."

"Wait one minute."

I could overhear talking and the male voice telling someone to tell Toy she had a call. Eventually, Toy picked up the phone.

"Hello."

"Toy, it's Jordan. I can hardly hear with all the music."

"You know how loud it gets in here...wait, let me close the door and get some privacy. Okay, this is better...I called you."

"Yeah, I got the message. I need to talk to you."

"You know I got a job tonight."

Talking in code, I said, "I understand. I'm in the city and wanted to come by and get something. Can you hook it up for me?"

"That'll be difficult...if my friend comes through here later, you want me to get something for you?"

"Yeah, that would be good. How 'bout an eight ball?" I said.

"Sure...but I can't promise you anything. Why don't you come by my place tomorrow, and I can score for you then?"

"Shit, I was hoping to get something today, but I guess I can hold out until tomorrow. What time?"

"Around seven or eight…okay?"

"That's fine."

"Don't my baby want to come see Mommy today? You're right here. I want to see you, sugar."

I smiled through the phone and said, "I need to leave the city early and have to do some things. We'll get together tomorrow… it'll be better then."

"So you could come by to get some fifty-one but not to see me?" Toy asked.

"Fifty-one?" I thought. "Must be another name for crack." I figured the experience of watching Toy undress in a booth with a Plexiglas barrier and retracting shade held no interest now that I had the real thing weeks before, so I declined the invitation. "Honey, I need to get back to work and back to Jersey. We'll do it tomorrow. Let me have a kiss," I said, waiting to hear a smack that never came through the phone.

"Call me tomorrow," Toy said.

"I will, but when you call my job, try to be nice. Use your last name, like Ms.…what's your last name, anyway?"

"My name is Towana Simmons. Toy is my stage name."

"Just say Ms. Simmons; I'll know who's calling."

"And you need to say sometin' to that bitch at your job…got all rude with me askin' questions and shit…I should have told her to kiss my ass."

"We'll talk when I see you, but that's my job, you know."

"I don't give a shit. She don't need to be gittin' all up in my business…that white bitch keeps askin' all these questions, like who's calling…what is this in reference to? Would you like him to call you back and shit."

"That's her job; she's my secretary," I said with a twinge of incredulousness.

"Well, you call me…I don't like all those questions, like the police or sometin'."

I couldn't take it any longer and brought the call to an end. "Got to run; have a good time tonight. I'll see you later…tomorrow."

"Okay, I'll see ya, sugar," Toy said.

"Wow, how crazy she is," I thought. "She has no idea about business or courtesy. She has the manners of the crowds stampeding into Wal-Mart on Black Friday.

I got to work about one and went straight to my desk, checked my messages, and took notice of the one from Nancy Reardon, the vice president of human resources. I was clueless as to what it was about. I rang Judy on the intercom and asked, "Do you know what this meeting at two with Nancy Reardon is all about?"

"I have no idea. When I asked her secretary, she said she wasn't sure."

"Okay."

I didn't think much about it and figured I'd find out soon enough. I went about my normal affairs, reviewing things in my in-box, and tried to focus as best I could. I didn't leave the office until time to go to the meeting in human resources.

At two I grabbed a notepad and headed to the meeting, taking the elevator to a lower floor. When I arrived, the door was closed, and the secretary told me, "Take a seat, Mr. Baros. Ms. Reardon will be right with you; she's speaking with Mr. Doran."

"Ted Doran," I thought. "Why is he here, and why didn't he inform me he was coming to this meeting? This is strange."

Before I could further deliberate the possibilities, the door opened. Nancy Reardon came out and said, "Jordan, you can join us now."

"Sure," I said, got up, and went into the office. Nancy showed me a seat on the other side of her small round conference table opposite to where Ted was sitting.

"Jordan, how are you?" Ted asked.

"I'm feeling better; I had an upset stomach this morning, nothing serious."

"Yes, there's a bug going around," Nancy said. "Glad to hear you're feeling better."

"Thank you," I said.

"I guess you're wondering what this is all about," Nancy said.

"Yes, I'm curious. The message I received didn't explain the purpose."

"Well, let me explain. I asked Ted to join us because this affects his department and you personally."

I looked directly at Ted, who avoided eye contact. The air was thick and stuffy; I sat straight up and leaned forward, quickly turning from Ted back to Nancy as she continued her preliminaries.

"We're making changes, and the Financial Services Section is being reorganized. The changes that are taking place in the business unit have resulted in the reassignment of some attorneys to other sections. Unfortunately, your job is being eliminated."

The only thing I could recall at that moment was the word *eliminated*, and I was stunned. "Be cool; don't let them see you sweat. How can they do this? These bastards," I thought.

"Now, don't take this personally; you have been a fine asset to the department, and we regret the changes that have to be made. Are there any questions?"

"What am I supposed to say? I come in, and I am told to report here without any idea what for...and now you tell me I'm fired... I'm stunned...unprepared and speechless."

"Take your time; I know this is difficult for you. It's difficult for us," Nancy said.

"You shouldn't take this personally, Jordan," Ted said. "You are an intelligent guy, and I'm sure you will find something more suitable."

"I don't know how else to take this but personally. Do you have any suggestions, Ted? I have to protect myself and my family, and I don't understand why this is happening."

"I had to make the hard decision; it's wasn't easy…it's my job as the head of the department," Ted said.

"I would like to know the criteria used to reach the decision."

There was a stony silence, and neither Nancy nor Ted responded to my question.

"You are entitled to severance of six weeks, all vacation time will be paid, and your last day will be next Friday. That will give you time to clean your office out, and we will provide outplacement assistance for six months…blah, blah, blah." Nancy continued with details that echoed off the walls. All I could think about was how I detested these two people. It was as if a sword pierced through my middle, and I was holding my intestines in place by wrapping my arms around the wounded area. This was the second time these people had attacked me. And now Ted was applying the lethal thrust.

When it was over, Nancy again expressed her regrets and stated that I should use the time before next Friday as I saw fit. Acting as if this was nothing more than a minor inconvenience, Ted said, "Sure, it might be best for you to take some time to yourself and come back next week to do whatever housecleaning needs doing."

After making his statement, Ted stood and extended his hand, which I refused. I nodded to both and left the office.

I didn't hang around after the meeting. Ironically, I felt relieved. It was unpleasant being there, and tolerance on both sides had waned, particularly after the treatment I received with the money-fund project. But faced with another trial, I also felt dejected, angry, alone, remorseful, pitiful, and aimless. In my present mental state, I knew I didn't have the fortitude to meet my challenges. I bought a crack pipe at a small smoke shop near Forty-Second Street that sold drug paraphernalia. I obsessed over the drug and figured I had a small stash at home but was concerned it was not enough to last until I saw Toy the next evening. The pain and obsession were too acute to take any chances. An addict easily succumbs to the compulsion of it all. I made a street purchase around Bryant Park. As I sat on the train, thoughts bombarded my mind like mortars during a fierce battle—the need to reconcile and win Trina back, sift the sewage I had thrown into our idyllic pond and family values, the breakup with Maria...wondering who was this new man in her life, what he did...how he looked—these thoughts were interspersed with getting high and needing a fix.

It was just before rush hour, and I had been able to find an empty seat on the train to gain some privacy. Settling in, I opened my package and looked at the chunks of light-brown hard crystalline rocks. I contemplated lighting up right there on the train. My rational self overcame the momentary impulse.

Once inside the sanctuary of home, I moved to an upstairs guest bedroom and prepared the "devil drug" by placing the rock at the filter end of the pipe and then held a flame underneath it and inhaled the vapors through the small glass tube. I could feel the sensation of the product being immediately absorbed into my bloodstream through my lungs. It made a direct hit on my brain. The amorphous feeling and lightness of being were exactly the prescription I needed. The new consciousness slayed the earlier depression and gave me a reprieve from the wretchedness prior to inhaling the potent elixir. I continued this affair throughout the evening and early morning, combining my drug consumption with alcohol and passing out on the floor half-dressed in the wee hours of the morning.

CHAPTER TWENTY-NINE

The roller coaster continued throughout the next day into the early evening until time to go to Toy's. I changed my wrinkled, disheveled clothes and put on all black: khaki pants, black hoodie, mock-turtleneck knit shirt, and Timberland boots. I got into the car and placed the crack pipe in the glove compartment. I had sealed the broken window from the last time I visited Toy with a transparent plastic bag and used duct tape to secure it. The wind crackled and snapped against the makeshift seal as I drove to Jersey City—the faster I drove, the noisier the snapping, and without a radio I could not offset the distraction. It was so unnerving that at one point, I envisioned flooring the car and running it into the concrete barrier on the highway, or better yet, careening through oncoming traffic on the other side of the highway and plunging into the sludge of the Passaic River. The thought of death was eerily comforting, and I smiled—the racket inside my tomb was silenced as I continued my drive through the industrial stench from the factories and refineries that lined the highway.

I entered Toy's building by pushing the front door with my shoulder. It was off its hinges and was unlocked and provided no form of security to the tenants inside. I climbed the steps to Toy's apartment and rang the bell.

"Who's that?"

"Jordan."

I waited as she disengaged the numerous locks on her door, finally letting me inside. She hid her body behind the door, poking her head from around the door to greet me.

"I was just getting in the shower," she said. Her body was now in full view as I closed the door behind me. She was wearing a short, silky robe to cover herself. I thought it interesting that she would display such modesty given everything I knew about her.

"Take a seat; I'll be right out," Toy said. She turned to go into the bathroom, and as she did, the robe rose up her backside, exposing her rear like a pair of Daisy Duke shorts. She reached back with her hand to brush the unruly part of her garment back in place as she disappeared into the bathroom and closed the door. I moved the clothes and papers on the futon to the side and sat down.

"Sweetie, look at my pictures I just got. See them on the table?" Toy yelled from the bathroom.

"Yeah, I see them."

A nicely bound portfolio was sitting on the table among the clutter. I looked at the photos that showed Toy in various sensuous poses, settings, and fashion accessories. Others were more private, showing her partially nude and covering her breasts with her hands or folded arms. Her makeup and hairpieces in some of the photos seemed a bit overdone; some of the pictures didn't even resemble Toy. I looked closer and harder to assure myself it was her.

"These are good. When did you take them?" I yelled.

"You like them? My friend, he's a photographer, took them," Toy shouted over the sound of the pitty-pat shower water hitting the porcelain tub.

When she finished, Toy came into the living room in her bra and panties, still wiping herself with a towel. The pictures and the live model in her underwear aroused me. I thought it interesting because I hadn't felt sexual when I arrived.

"Yeah, my friend is a photographer, and he took them," she said, repeating herself.

"They are nice. What are they for?"

"I do modeling; this is my portfolio."

"Have you done anything I've seen?"

"Yeah, some cigarette and liquor commercials; they're all magazine shots. *Ebony, Jet, Emerge* magazines."

"That's great. I didn't know you're a star."

"Yeah, but it's hard. They criticize you and everything...they say I'm too heavy for fashion and runway. Magazines don't pay you nothin'. And all these dudes out here promise you shit and stuff, and they ain't bout nothin' but tryin' to screw you and take your money. But I'm gonna keep tryin' and make sometin' happen."

"Well, it looks good. You need to get with the right people...a good agent in the business, and let them put your stuff out there. I can be your lawyer," I said, trying to be encouraging.

"You know some people in the music or fashion business?"

"No, I don't, but I'll talk to people and see if I can get you some names."

"That's sweet. That would be good. You know what else I want to do?" Toy was excited, her eyes sparkling like a child on Christmas morning, opening gifts under the tree. "I want to go to Fashion Institute of Technology and study fashion design."

I understood her excitement and hope for a meaningful life, a desire for respect and accomplishment. Passion to achieve laced her statements. But I also knew from an earlier conversation that she had never completed high school, was pregnant at sixteen, and failed to get her GED.

"That would be great, and you would be good at it. That's a goal you need to pursue," I said, not wanting to discourage her pipe dreams.

"Let me go put on some clothes, and then we can go downstairs. I need a hit…but I should stop…maybe tomorrow," she said.

"You want me to go with you?"

"Yeah, it's cool. I know them. It's Trea and his friends and probably some other folks who hang out there. It'll be okay."

"You sure? I don't know about that," I said, feeling reluctant about going into a crack den and sitting down with them as a buyer.

"You be wit' me…it's cool."

Toy changed into a tight-fitting pair of jeans, heels, and a thin white sports T-shirt, her hair falling loosely on her shoulders. She had rouge on her cheeks and gloss on her lips, and she wore gold hoop earrings. She looked cute and fresh.

"Ready. How do I look?"

"You look good. Gimme a kiss."

She moved up to me and turned her cheek so that I could place a kiss there. I obliged by licking the side of her face.

"Ooouuu, you nasty," Toy said as she wiggled while in my arms in playful disgust. "We better go before I rape you."

"Why did you turn your cheek to me?"

"I don't want you to mess up my makeup, honey. You can mess me up later, baby, if you want."

"You are too much, Ms. Simmons."

We went downstairs to the first floor apartment Toy had entered that first night we were together. A makeshift slot had been cut into the door, of the apartment and when Toy rang the bell, a gravelly voice as deep and gritty as that of DMX came through the opened slot from inside.

"Who is it?"

"It's Toy, Brinks…let me in."

"How do I know it's you?"

"Nigga, if you don't open this door, I am gonna break it down and kick your ass. Then I bet you'll know who it is."

There was a gruff laugh from inside, and the door opened.

"I knew it was you. You know I like to fuck with you. How you doin', baby?" said a short broad man with no neck. His whole body looked like one hard muscle, a pugnacious bulldog of a man. He had the complexion of an iron frying pan and a prominent scar from a razor or knife on his left cheek, a bald head, and a Kool menthol cigarette dangling from his mouth as if it was permanently placed there.

I was standing behind Toy and moved to her side.

"Brinks, this is my friend, Jordan. He's a lawyer."

"Damn! What did she go and say that for?" I thought. "This man probably hates lawyers and cops."

"You a lawyer?" Brinks said. The stern, intimidating voice that I had initially heard had returned.

"Yeah, I do business law."

"You sure you not Five-o?" he said.

"What?" I said, not immediately comprehending the slang term for *cop*.

"You can't hear, muthafucka?"

"Shuddup, Brinks, and leave my friend alone," Toy moved in to say.

"Just checkin' my man—you know how it is," Brinks said as he extended his hand with a mangled index finger that was lumpy and crooked, cocked his head, and looked up at me. My hand was engulfed in Brinks's grip, and he applied pressure that made me realize I had lost the first round. This was Brinks's territory, and he was in charge. I later found out Brinks had gotten his name as the result of a robbery attempt of an armored car when he was a teenager. His trigger finger had been damaged when the gun backfired. He had a long prison record.

"Where's Trea?" Toy asked.

"He's in the back with Dashawn and Rasheed. Some other folks in the back doin' their thing."

"You not packin', are you, my man?" Brinks asked me.

"No," I said, catching myself before I said "sir."

"Let me just check you," he said. He began to pat me down with the hand that had that mangled finger, with particular concentration around my crotch.

I looked at Toy, who returned a helpless stare, as if there was nothing she could do. "Brinks, are you finished now? Can we go? Damn nigga. You act like this is Fort Knox."

"Yeah, baby, you can go. You know the deal…what you want me to do?"

"I know, sugar, but he's cool. Trust me."

"I do, baby. You my girl, and all this is just business," he said, whistling his *s*'s as he spoke. "You okay, lawyer man. You know how it is…go on in the back there. My man'll take care o' y'all."

"Phew," I thought. "This checkpoint is like something in a war zone."

"Sure, man. I understand," I said, trying to sound more confident than I had earlier.

Toy and I walked down a long hallway toward the kitchen. I followed behind the tap-dance clicks of Toy's stiletto heels on the hardwood flooring. The sweet smell of jasmine incense clashed with the sensory expectation of something more akin to molting iron in the pits of hell.

There were rooms that flowed off the hallway. One had its door closed. Another dimly lit room was occupied, but it was difficult to see who was in there or what was going on. I stepped fully into what looked like a dining-room area converted to a meeting room. There was a dining-room table with folding chairs around it and others against the wall. There were people in the room. At the head of the table was a highly varnished high-back wicker chair of the Huey Newton motif. A man was sitting in it with his legs crossed; he had a flat-top Afro with faded sides.

"Hey, baby," a white woman said as she entered from an adjoining bedroom. She was smoking a joint and was dressed in a trashy miniskirt and small midriff halter top that hugged her braless breasts like cellophane and gave prominence to her large nipples.

"Hi, Shonda. This is Jordan; he's my friend."

"Thank God she didn't introduce me as a lawyer," I said to myself.

"Hey, Jordan," Shonda said, involuntarily lowering her eyes to check out my private parts as she spoke.

"Whasupwityou, pretty girl? You not gonna recognize me?" the man sitting at the head of the table in the wicker chair shouted. He looked awfully familiar to me.

"Yeah, whasupwitdat?" a chorus of voices added from the other men at the table.

"Shuddup, Trea," Toy said to him as he stood to his full six-foot-four, two-hundred-and-twenty-five-pound frame. She disappeared in his embrace, reappearing once he opened his arms. She greeted and kissed each of the other men and called them by name—Dashawn and Rasheed.

"Hey, man, how you doin'?" Trea said to me as he approached, extending his hand to try to give me a power handshake. I confused the pattern and motion but completed the ritual the best I could.

"What's happenin'?" Rasheed said, looking up while remaining in his seat and not offering to shake my hand.

Dashawn didn't look up; he mumbled something and nodded his head. Shonda left the room without saying more, and Trea resumed his seat at the head of the table. I instinctively knew that Trea was the alpha male and leader of the posse. He looked like the only one who could beat Brinks or at least hold him until back-up came.

Toy and I took seats at the table. Toy sat closer to Trea.

"How are things, baby? You lookin' good as usual," Trea said to Toy.

"Things are cool. Keepin' it on the up and up."

Trea lit a pipe while the small talk between Toy and the crew was going on and passed it to me.

The gesture relieved some of the stress Brinks had caused, and I absorbed a hit into my body.

"So what's your story?" Trea asked me.

"I, ah—" Before I could finish, Toy, who had also taken a hit, passed the pipe along and interrupted.

"He's a lawyer; he's helpin' me with my modeling career."

"Is that for sure?" Trea asked.

"Well, I think she's got potential, the right people behind her... you never know."

Rasheed and Dashawn said nothing at this point, waiting for Trea to follow up.

Changing the direction of the conversation, he said, "I'm thinking about doin' a law thing myself. I know somebody at college who's gonna hook me up. You know James Street? They call him Street."

"No, I don't know him. What college is that?"

"It's in New York—Manhattan Community. He's my PO's brother."

I figured Trea didn't have a clue about what being a lawyer entailed, but I was not about to challenge or embarrass him with details about college degrees, three years of graduate school, bar exams, and the requirement of having no felony record. The bigger issue was that I now recognized him as someone I had prosecuted years ago when I was a DA out of law school. The details of the conviction escaped me. However, the awareness of having faced Trea in court heightened my anxiety. I hoped that Trea wouldn't recognize me as one of the people who contributed to his rap sheet and preventing his dream of going to law school.

"That sounds good. I've been practicing for about eight years," I said.

"I got this thing hangin' over me from some time ago. Maybe you can help straighten it out. A friend told me they can erase things off your record...forget what they call it."

"Expungement," I said, wishing Trea would stop all this legal talk.

Without any advance warning, a loud bark came from a bedroom off the dining room and caused me to jump. Trea yelled back as loud as the pit bull's bark, "Shuddup, Bullet!" A dog that was chained to the radiator cowered back to its original prone position before the bark. Trea got up to let the dog loose, and it scurried into the room to a gnawed ham bone on the floor in the corner and then back to Trea, who held it by a tight choker leash as it lounged playfully at Rasheed, who was sitting on the other side of the table opposite me. The dog slobbered on his army-fatigue-pants leg. The dog was built like Brinks—a muscle—but was wrapped in fur.

Feeling more and more uncomfortable, I whispered to Toy while Trea was involved with Bullet to make the buy so we could leave.

"So listen, baby, my friend wants to cop some devil. Can you do that for him?" Toy asked Trea.

"Can I do that? What are you asking? You know I got the stuff. You got the cake? I just need some finance before I can give you the romance," Trea said in his most poetic rap.

"How much, Jordan?" Toy said.

"An eight ball is fine."

"Sure you don't want no more than that? This is some good shit I got. I can shoot you a *G* for a good price, Mr. Big-Time Attorney."

"I can't do that much tonight but maybe next time," I said, assuming a *G* to be a large amount.

"Ain't this a merry muthafucka. I can't promise you'll be able to do this next time; I got to move this shit…you a big man. You don't need to be nickel and diming. You look familiar to me, man… where you from?"

I was in too deep. I barely understood what Trea had just said, but I replied, "I'm not from around here." I lied, saying I was from Ohio, where I went to school, to try to deflect his memory.

"Trea, he's only getting somethin' for now. Don't be tryin' to push any more on him. The shit is cool; he gittin' it for me and him for the weekend," Toy said.

Trea turned his attention to Toy. "You need to watch yourself, Toy; you gonna turn into some crackhead skeezer bitch, you keep hittin' this pipe."

Dashawn and Rasheed were both looking at Toy and shaking their heads like two bobblehead dolls.

Toy looked at Trea, extending her neck and flailing both her hands while speaking, like I had witnessed before. "I know what I'm doin'! Don't worry 'bout me. Ain't none o' you niggas paying my bills or getting' any of this honey without some money."

"Slow down, baby, no disrespect," Trea said. "You know how much I love you…baby, slow ya roll." He smiled at Toy, who seductively lowered her eyes, like a little girl receiving a compliment from her father.

"Dashawn, take my man in the room and fix him up. Toy, come with me; I need to talk to you 'bout somethin'," Trea said abruptly, signifying that the meeting was over.

Hesitating at first and looking at Toy, who said to go ahead, I went with Dashawn to the bedroom with the closed door, the one Toy and I had passed on the way to the converted dining room. Once inside, Dashawn entered a code to a safe on the floor and opened the door, pulling out a plastic bag that held the quantity

I asked for. I looked in the safe and saw some automatic weapons and a substantial amount of packaged drugs and cash.

Showing the contents to me so I could see the goods, he said, "It's two-fifty."

"I thought it was two hundred," I said, referring to the price Toy had quoted.

"What the fuck are you talkin' 'bout?" Dashawn said, frowning and looking me in the eye while pulling open his leather coat to show the pistol in his belt. "You want it or not?"

"Yeah, no problem," I responded, having lost another round in a world in which I was completely alien.

"Lucky I got that much on me," I said, and I thought, "Somebody's ripping me off and making an additional fifty bucks, but I can't challenge the pricing. And who am I going to complain to—the Better Business Bureau?"

"Yeah, lucky for who…you or me?"

"I was just, ah—"

"I don't need all that bullshit…take the shit," Dashawn said indignantly as he handed me the bag of drugs and grabbed the money. He then turned his back and bent down to close the safe.

I was angry but quickly dismissed the thought of hitting this wretched creature on the back of his neck taking his gun and shooting him in the ass. I knew there was no recourse to Dashawn's dismissive attitude, so I left the room to go back and get Toy.

"Where's Toy?" I asked Rasheed.

"She's with Trea in the room," he said, pointing to the room where the pit bull was. Its door was closed. I started to walk toward the room, and Rasheed got up. He was my height, and we faced off as he blocked my movement.

"I don't think you want to do that. You got your stuff, right? Maybe you should leave. I'll tell Toy you left, okay?"

"Look, man, can you let her know I'm leaving?"

Rasheed obliged and yelled through the door, "Toy, your friend says good-bye."

Hearing no reply, Rasheed shrugged his shoulders and gestured for me to leave. I had no clue what was happening but realized I had no options, and it was in my best interest to leave. I hurriedly made my way out of the apartment and reached the front entrance, where Brinks stood guard.

"Yo, my man…Mr. Lawyer…let me whisper sometin' in your ear," Brinks said, gesturing for me to lower my head, which I instinctively did. "I got this hard dick between my legs for you to suck…you kno what I'm sayin'?"

I pulled back, wondering if I heard right. This Mike Tyson–looking character with the sociopathic scowl that could make the hardest thugs pee in their pants…was gay!

"I don't go there," I managed to say.

"Half the motherfuckas I make suck my dick say the same thing, partna."

"I got to go. Can you open the door?" I asked, with my voice trembling and my tongue overburdened as I forced the request out of my mouth.

"Don't worry, man. I ain't gonna fuck you today…ya know what I'm sayin'? You take care, my man," he said, unlocking the security devices and chains on the door. Laughing demonically, he asked if I had a business card. I ignored him and continued walking out the door.

CHAPTER THIRTY

I reached the car in a state of psychological meltdown. The experience had exacerbated my fragility, and I was emasculated from the encounter. After sitting in the car trying to regain composure, I banged my head on the steering wheel and stopped in sheer terror when I imagined that Brinks was in the backseat with a gun at my head. Looking in the back and seeing no one didn't convince me there was no threat.

I quickly opened the glove compartment, removed the glass pipe, got out of the car, and walked toward Jackson Avenue at a brisk pace. I occasionally looked over my shoulder, checking to see if Brinks was following. I walked down a desolate, dark side street with abandoned buildings and broken-out streetlights and stopped in front of two abandoned buildings next to a vacant lot. I sought refuge and entered a driveway between the buildings. I walked through the strewn garbage and debris, making my way to the backyard of one of the buildings. There was an abandoned Chevy Impala on cinder blocks in the back with a striped alley cat perched on the car's hood that meowed at my intrusion. The

stench smelled like soured milk. Rodents jumped and scurried between the garbage and debris, at times crossing over my feet as I
took a seat on the broken concrete back stoop that was crumbling
and decimated by weather and human neglect.

Feeling secure after eluding the Brinks phantom, I prepared
my sedative to infuse its healing powers into my body. I smoked
and was drawn into a transcendental resurrection. "Fuck those
bastards," I thought. "Who do they think they are? I need to help
Toy before it's too late. They will probably gangbang her." I took
another toke as the vermin poked their heads up from the debris,
with glaring iridescent eyes piercing the darkness where they re-
sided. Frustrated and unconcerned, oblivious to fear and personal
safety, my mind raced from one issue to another. Eventually I left
the stoop and stealthily moved back to the car.

"Brinks is probably not there now. If I can get in an escape
before he returns…need to stop by Maria's to see her before I go
home; she needs to know what's happening. People may try to
harm her. I need to let her know what's happening…I can't help
Toy, but it's not too late for Maria," I told myself.

"You need to quit."

"Stop the pain."

"Peace in death."

"You whimpering punk."

"Clown, nigga, faggot."

The unrelenting choir of voices rejoiced in unison about their
unanimous sentence of my fate. I drove through the Holland
Tunnel, headed to Brooklyn. The drive was an eternity of infinite
darkness, like a black hole that prevented me from conceptualiz-
ing if it would end or vanquish me with its bleakness.

I reached Maria's block and parked the car with a clear view of
her apartment. Sitting there, I grabbed the package containing the
rocks, lit the pipe, and inhaled the vapors. I felt the top of my head
open up to release the noise to make room for the exhilaration of

the rush and the dismantling of my essence by Lucifer's disciple. I smoked and waited.

Eventually I walked to the building and rang the bell. There was no answer, so I rang the bell of other apartments until someone responded, and I gained entrance. Once upstairs, I sat down in the hallway beside Maria's door to wait for her return. She never appeared. After some time passed, I went back to the car and continued waiting.

"My enemies are trying to destroy me…those racist, double-crossing bastards at Federal…they sabotaged me…Maria will probably cook for us, and we'll make love like before…she will be so happy to see me," I thought, vacillating between anger, fantasy, and sedation.

Finally, after hours, I left the car to find a payphone. I called Maria and left a message. "I need to talk to you. It's urgent; please call me as soon as possible." After satisfying my mission, I drove away, headed back home, certain she would call and angry at her for not being there when I needed her.

CHAPTER THIRTY-ONE

I can't explain how I got home that early morning because I don't know. I remember at one point pulling to the side of the highway, incapable of controlling my bodily functions, and I defecated and urinated on myself. Once I regained consciousness, I continued my trek. I could not accept my failings. I spent the weekend in self-flagellation and self-pity. Paranoid thoughts overwhelmed me. Naked and unclean, I thought others were looking through the windows, so I covered them with sheets and crouched in a corner to smoke crack. At one time, I thought I was covered with ants that sought to enter my body through my mouth, eyes, nose, ears, penis, and anus. I showered to remove them and fell in the bathroom, hitting my head on the side of the tub. I lay there unconscious and bleeding. The drug no longer helped deflect the condition or mask the symptoms—it made the ominous voices louder. The more I indulged, the louder they became, and the deeper I sank.

The end seemed inevitable. When I accepted this fate, the voices became less shrill, like whispers in the wind. A strange counterforce surfaced at my weakest point in a desperate effort to fight back the evil that had overtaken me. Instinctively driven by self-preservation and need for order in my chaotic state, I started to clean the house, meticulously scrubbing the bathroom, washing the dishes, applying solvents to the countertops and oven, vacuuming, and dusting. I placed the soiled clothes in the wash. I discarded the packages of crack cocaine and glass pipe, placing them in the garbage and carrying everything outside to the trash.

I laid on the bed my navy-blue suit, crisp white shirt, red tie and placed my Johnston & Murphy black wingtips below on the floor—the same attire I wore when presenting to the Federal Board months before. I continued to obsess with order and cleanliness, and the voices remained a distant inaudible murmur. Again, I entered the shower and cleansed my body thoroughly.

But the good forces diminished as quickly as they had emerged. After putting on my suit and tie, I took from the shelf behind the clothes in Trina's closet a green tin box I had placed there years ago. Trina had urged me to do this as the kids got older; she feared that they might find it under the bed and do harm. I removed the key from an envelope in the top drawer of my dresser, placed it in my suit pocket, and carried the green tin to the home office across the hallway. After entering the room, I calmly sat at the desk and tried once more to muster hope and reason for living to offset my sinking depression and suicidal urges. It was to no avail.

Providentially, a vision appeared, and the negative voices were replaced with inspiration. I imagined being at rest in a cathedral-domed church, lying in a coffin with a black choir all dressed in white, singing gospel hymns. Bouquets of multicolored flowers were all around, the floral scent pervading the air and uplifting the celestial spirits of those attending. They all stood in the back of the church, and I could not make out who was there as they gazed from a distance. Slowly, a selection of those gathered came forward, one at a time: Trina, Chad, Jared, my mother, Tom, Wanda, Maria, Stacey, Carmen, June, the father I never knew, Hazel and

George, grandparents, cousins, relatives, and friends. They grieved and cried and expressed their love and admiration. Through a vision of death, I imagined a communion of happiness I had not attained in this life.

The vision faded and I removed the key from my pocket, inserted it into the green tin box, removed the fully loaded .25-caliber handgun, released the safety, and placed the instrument to my head. I imagined a sound I would never hear. The voices ceased, my muscles relaxed, and my head fell to the desk. The pain subsided and left my body.

CHAPTER THIRTY-TWO

I picked up the ringing phone, unaware if I was dreaming or awake, just that I heard an annoying ring and wanted it to stop.

"Hello," I said into the phone.

"Jordan, what's going on?" Trina asked. "I've been calling for the last few days. Are you okay?"

"Yeah...why? What's...the matter?" I replied, still in a suspended state of drugs and surrealism.

"Did you get my message? I called Wednesday to remind you of Chad's game Thursday. I needed you to take him; I couldn't get away from work. Did you get the message?"

"What day is it?"

"It's Saturday. Are you all right? You sound out of it."

"I was asleep, and a lot has happened. When was the game?"

"It was Thursday...I just said. Chad asked for you. My mother and dad took him; you should have been there."

"I'm sorry," I said, feeling like I had been dowsed with cold water and was now more alert, trying to keep pace with Trina's ranting. "I lost my job."

"What! Oh my God, what happened?"

"I told you things were bad after the presentation. I figured this might happen. I don't care; I'll get another job."

"I'm so sorry to hear that. Anything you want me to do?"

"About that, no, but I need help. I'm not doing well."

"What do you mean?"

"I've got a problem. I need to see someone. I've been drinking, depressed, and down. I can't help myself. Ever since you left, everything has fallen apart."

"I've thought about things since we last talked, and I want us to try to work on our relationship. The boys need their father, and I need you. I'm hurting also. I will be over to get you, okay?"

"I apologize, Trina. I hate for you to see me like this. I'll see you when you get here." After hanging up, I felt a gleam of light for the first time in a while. The years of duplicity, lies, and self-denial had cascaded over a crest, like a waterfall into reality. In the past, when confronted, I asked myself, "Was this what I really wanted? Was I ready to stop what I was doing? Can I renew my vows to Trina?" Those questions were no longer relevant.

The ugliness of the days before was still in the house, but I put the weapon away, locked the box, and waited for Trina to arrive.

CHAPTER THIRTY-THREE

It was ten thirty when Trina arrived. I met her at the door, and she looked fresh in casual designer jeans, a red cashmere sweater, and a lightweight leather spring jacket.

The first thing she said was, "What happened to you? You look terrible. You have dark circles around your eyes. Are you sick?"

"I'll tell you later. Where are we going?"

"It's a surprise, but you can't go like that," she said, looking me up and down. I had changed into some baggy sweats and a loose-fitting wool sweater and sneaks.

Taking me by the hand, she led me up the stairs to my closet. "The house is so clean. Did you have someone come clean? Has June been here since I left?"

"No. You know me and my OCD."

"Well, it looks good. We need to get you lookin' better," she said, scolding me again, unaware of how close I was to having a nervous breakdown. She picked out a pair of black pants, a matching crew-neck sweater, a gray striped shirt, and dress shoes.

"You still haven't told me where we're going," I said.

"Good things come to those who wait," she told me. We left the house, and I followed Trina. She was in charge.

━╬╬━

"Remember the Charles Alston exhibit I mentioned for us to see? Well, here we are. After our creative stimulation, we can go talk about some more serious things. You like?"

"Yes, surprised. I forgot about this. Nice, a Saturday in the Village with you, déjà vu, nice one."

The gallery, a large former shoe factory, was divided by constructed gypsum walls on the first floor to separate the exhibits. The architect had skillfully incorporated salvaged and retro materials into the modern design. The dominant color was pure white except for the multihued exhibits and restored yellow-pine hardwood floors. The halogen track lighting added even more brightness to the interior. The Alston collection occupied the entire second floor at the top of a white steel stairwell that looked as if it had been a fire escape in a previous life.

"What a large collection," I said.

"He was a prolific artist, but critics claim he never established a signature style," Trina said.

We started to view the works, when a woman approached who introduced herself as the gallery's director. She gave us a brief orientation to Charles Alston and his paintings.

"Feel free to ask any questions of me or any of my assistants; they are stationed throughout the gallery," she said as she handed us a brochure that further described the exhibit.

There were a number of impressive pieces, such as *Blues Song*, which demonstrated Alston's sculptural values in portraying the musicians and entertainers in Harlem during the 1930s. He loved and hung out with these so-called real people, akin to the "keeping it real" mantra of today. Another interesting painting was titled

Black Man; Black Woman, USA. Alston derived the inspiration from Ralph Ellison's book *Invisible Man.* It featured a young black couple sitting regally in a high-back, throne-like bench, but with featureless faces. Trina recalled reading somewhere that Alston told of an incident that confirmed the message of the painting.

"He was at a party and met an elderly white woman who wanted to demonstrate her racial color blindness and liberal persuasion… she told him that her cook, Cora, who had served her family for decades, was just like a member of the family. Having heard these kinds of stories countless times, Alston asked the woman, 'What's Cora's last name?' The woman did not know it. Like Ellison, he depicted the facelessness of black people—one did it in literature, the other in paintings."

"Damn, girl, you know your shit!" I said, complimenting Trina.

One painting carried significance for both of us; it was titled *Family No. 1.* It was one of a series of paintings that expressed Alston's relationship and ties to his family roots and the larger caring and spiritual tradition of black families in spite of poverty and discrimination. We sat on the gallery bench facing the painting that showed a family of four—husband, wife, and two children—and processed the image and its application to our lives and present trial.

"This is a masterful piece, and he captures the inner strength of the unity of family," Trina said.

"Yeah, look at that size of the characters, all tightly bound together on the canvas, with their elongated necks."

"Some strong African and Mexican Cubist influence on the form and volume…I love it!" Trina exclaimed.

Hours later, fulfilled with the beautiful black visions and history of the Alston exhibit as well as others, we decided to go to a café in the lower level of the gallery.

"I enjoyed that. Alston was an influential artist who never got the recognition I think he deserved," I said.

"Please—so much talent has gone unnoticed over the years because of race. It's disgusting," Trina said.

"Honey, this was great, just what I needed. But I need to tell you something," I started, but then I hesitated and bowed my head.

"What are you getting ready to tell me? Somebody pregnant?"

"What? No. Worse. I'm an addict. It has gotten worse since you left, and I have reached a low point."

"You've always smoked, and I know you do coke. We both do; it's recreational, fun, at least for me," Trina said.

"I've been smoking crack for a while now, drinking, smoking weed, whatever, to numb myself."

"Crack cocaine—when did you do that?"

"I started after you left, a while ago. I smoked with a friend, and with all that's been happening, I've just lost it. The reason I didn't answer the phone is that I've been stuck in the house getting high. It's affected everything, even my health. Once I lost the job, the bottom fell out. I need to detox and get counseling."

"What friend? Somebody I know? Oh my God…well, they say the first step to recovery is admission and a cry for help. I don't believe you. How do you go from corporate lawyer and family to this? Maybe your problem is deeper than you think; your addiction isn't just drugs."

"Yeah, I know it's deep. I need serious therapy."

"You have always had trauma related to childhood. There's this hole in your heart that needs to be filled. It's what concerns me most about you. Can anyone fill that hole? Maybe you need a holistic approach, something that looks at your whole life. But you've got to stop the drug craving first and then do the other stuff."

"I know. First thing next week, I'm going to start rehab."

Trina didn't say anything for what seemed like hours, just staring at me, expressionless.

"What are you thinking?" I asked.

"Wondering why I still love you. You left me, I have never left you, and I still want to be with you. Am I crazy?"

"No," I said and exhaled a sigh of relief.

She murmured under her breath, loud enough for me to hear, "Crack!?"

We ordered sandwiches and coffee and sat there quietly contemplating what had just been said.

Trina was the first to speak again after another pause. "Your problem is not long-term addiction. Hopefully, you have come to your senses and put this behind you. Can we talk about some other things?" Before I could respond, she said, "I would love to buy the *Family* painting. It was a copy with Alston's original signature and costs five thousand dollars."

"It's not that expensive and may be an investment, considering future value," I offered.

"What do you mean?"

"Well, he's a recognized painter. I also saw that he is related through marriage to Romare Bearden, whom he tutored. And you said he mentored Jacob Lawrence—what more do you want?"

"If we get back together, I'll pay my share. You know I'm a working woman now. We can go sixty percent you and forty percent me...that's fair. I love it. He had a recurring theme of family in a lot of his works...it was nice and symbolic, with all the stuff we're going through."

"If? You have to trust me again. I want us to be a family. I apologize for all the hurt I've caused. You have to give me a chance to make it up...prove myself. I'm going to straighten up. You'll see, but I need you to do it."

"You know what my problem is?" Trina said. "I'm always the last one to the party. Finally, I've been able to take on a good job with responsibility and a decent salary. The women I know my age did the career thing early or had the good sense to know it wasn't for them. But I was naïve, immature in many ways. I lost out, and now I'm still losing. I'm always behind, out of step, can't measure up—no matter how hard I try. I don't know how to explain it, but it's like not being respected. I guess my insecurities have always held me back, real and imagined. Some people take advantage of my weaknesses, my naïveté. They even take my man...Jesus, what the fuck. Even you, my best friend, I'm always trying to prove to you that I'm worthy...that I'm good enough. When you were in law school, I felt so inadequate...like a nothing. You would talk about other women as if they were so great. After I got pregnant with Jared, I had to abandon my plans for graduate school, and I gained weight and felt worse than ever. You found an attractive, glamorous, New York working woman. I just can't keep up...I don't know what I do wrong."

I listened to everything Trina said without responding, continuing to share her pain. She asked me, "Do you hear me? Am I rambling? Does this make sense to you?"

"Yes, yes. I hear everything you're saying and feel your pain... really, I do. I've tried to be supportive, but yes, I failed you, as a best friend and as a husband, and I know how you are hurting. I listen to you, and I witness your struggles, but you are different and still young; you are someone with options. You're intelligent and attractive. One thing I think is that Hazel's dominance has affected you more than anything. She sheltered you from taking risks...falling in love, getting your heart broken, bouncing back, and learning who you are, your strengths and weaknesses. Exposing yourself allows you to develop emotional stability and locus of control. Not that that's what I want you to do now, but if you had rebelled a little bit against your mother's control, maybe the questions you have would have been answered. You left George and Hazel and married me. Don't get me wrong; I wanted you because of the innocence...purity. I know you love me, and that is so important to me...but in spite of that, I compete for your love and attention because of your needs, the unfinished portion that drives you. We have created emotional silos for ourselves."

"You think I have low self-esteem?" Trina asked.

"Maybe, yes, in some ways. Look, you're accomplished, a mother, wife, educated. You're starting to build a great career. You grew up in privilege, different from me. I used to envy you; things you take for granted blew my mind. You are accustomed to material things. Nice clothes, travel. I think your highs and lows are tied to things. In your world, that's just the way it is. In my world, a lack of things built self-reliance and fortitude. We all have limitations; trust me—we can both do better by each other. Learn to instinctively respond to the other, not have to be told, true soulmates, empathy, compassion, and selflessness."

"I hear you, baby, and I do appreciate all you've done. You are a good man, a good provider, and maybe I don't always tell you that as often as you deserve. But you have to return the compliment when I come home from work—fix dinner, do homework with Jared, and pick up behind all of you. When was the last time you said 'thank you' for a meal I prepared? And how many times have I prepared dinner to have you call and say you'll be late or you'll get something while you're out...probably out having dinner with one of your women. But forget that. Let's put that aside and behind. I envy you...you are able to dream and visualize a different kind of life with someone else, but I can't travel that road because it would be pure fantasy.

"Also, I can't deny us this chance. We are young enough to turn this around, if this is what we really want. We only get one life, and if we are miserable apart and have the will to make it work, let's do what's necessary. The things you say about the void in our marriage have been said many times before. Life without you will be difficult, if not impossible, but during this separation, I have accepted that if you don't want me anymore, then I don't want to continue this charade. I desperately want us to be together, but only if you can return the love I have for you…and be happy."

There were no tears this time, just a steely strength and defined thoughts about our future. I reached out to hold her hand, but that was not what she wanted, and she pulled it back.

"Let me finish; this is so hard for me to say. I'm sorry, but I don't think it will ever be the way it was. Trust and loyalty are so important to me, particularly when it has been so difficult to come by. I placed too much faith in you, and you destroyed that faith… how can I ever trust you again?"

"I know. And I hear you, everything you've said. It just wasn't supposed to be this way. For two people who are bright and intelligent with two great kids and seemingly everything going for them—why is it so difficult? I don't want to lose it. You have to believe me. I will do whatever it takes to get you and the boys back."

"That's the problem, Jordan; I don't know how to answer you. What does 'whatever it takes' mean? It was much easier when you vowed to love and cherish me until death do us part; now I'm not sure. I know you are a nonbeliever, an agnostic, you say, and I don't pressure you about religion. But we should embrace a philosophy together that has roots and bearings that can give us guidance. Let's not make it up on the run. You know what I'm saying? I think you will enjoy the minister at the church I'm attending. It's a nondenominational church, communal in spirit, not a cult like Scientology and that stuff. He preached last week about Saint Augustine and discussed the good and evil in us. Did you know Augustine was African?"

"No, not really."

"Yes. He was one of Christianity's most important philosophers. The minister spoke of the conflicts with material and physical pleasures to the destruction of self and the greater good embodied in allowing Christ into our lives. Saint Augustine is an inspiration because of his loose living as a young man and complete conversion later. Christ represents the standard we aspire to for our happiness and worth. He also talked about the body and soul of marriage between man and woman for the wholeness of life on earth. As I listened, it came to me that this is us, our kids, our journey, and its legacy. I don't want us to waste this gift we have. That's why I'm so angry with you."

"Damn, Trina, you continue to amaze me. I'm willing to try, and I'm not an atheist, I don't think. I just have my doubts, but I need to open up and be less cynical—I will give you that. Yes, I will go with you. I want to hear this minister; he sounds interesting."

"You promise you'll go?"

I got up, walked around the table as she stood up, and put my arms around her shoulders. She looked up, and we softly touched lips.

"It's time to go," I said. "We need to buy that painting and get home so I can hug those boys."

www.ingramcontent.com/pod-product-compliance
Lightning Source LLC
Chambersburg PA
CBHW031306120626
46554CB00001BA/301